AWAKEN

AWAKEN

a novel

by

Denese Shelton

SHE WRITES PRESS

Published July 10, 2018
Printed in the United States of America
Print ISBN: 978-1-63152-363-2
E-ISBN: 978-1-63152-364-9
Library of Congress Control Number: 2018930493

Book design by Stacey Aaronson

For information, address:
She Writes Press
1563 Solano Ave #546
Berkeley, CA 94707

She Writes Press is a division of SparkPoint Studio, LLC.

This book is dedicated to love
and everyone who believes in love in all its forms.

Chapter 1

*N*ow I lay me down to sleep. I pray the Lord my soul to keep. If I should die before I wake, I pray the Lord my soul to take."

Sierra Harper whispered the prayer as she lay in bed, hoping tonight would be the night when she would be dreamless—or if not dreamless, at least full of harmless dreams. This was the first prayer she remembered learning, and after a long hibernation, it had managed to push its way to the forefront of her mind and out of her mouth as she tossed her way through another sleepless night.

She let out the breath she was unconsciously holding and turned toward the window in her bedroom. The blinds were closed and let in only a sliver of light. She had closed them hoping the darkness would help block out images that would cause her to think about anything at all. Perhaps if her mind were blank, she thought, the dreams wouldn't come.

For a moment, she looked at the clock. It was 3:00 a.m. She didn't have a lot of time left to even attempt some rest; soon, she would have to get up and get ready for work.

"All right, I need to at least try to sleep," she said aloud, and she began to count sheep in her head. Although sheep were cliché, she hoped that the simplicity of the exercise would put her into a peaceful slumber.

Slowly but surely, Sierra's eyes became heavy. She was asleep . . . and then she was awake.

⁓

Sierra was running. It was dark. The soil and rocks beneath her feet cut and bruised her skin with each stride, but she kept on running. She had to.

The night air was cold. Her lean body felt stiff from the chill, and her muscles wanted to lock up. She'd been running for so long. She could hear the dogs somewhere behind her, barking viciously, and the primal screams of the hunters. They were getting closer. She was running out of time, out of place, out of life.

"God, please, help me," she begged.

She couldn't remember what she'd done to incite this chase. She didn't know if she was a thief, a robber, or just disobedient. She had a vague recollection of an accusation, an argument, and a quilt. But nothing made any sense right now.

Sierra looked down at her hands and saw that she wasn't carrying anything but herself. Yet she sensed that the weight, the burden, of being, of existing in this life that she was running from, was beginning to take its toll. Her face dripping with sweat, she passed trees and figures in the abyss of the night that she could scarcely make out, and still she ran on.

The whiteness of her dress screeched against the sinister

darkness of the night. If she were naked, she thought, the night would welcome her into its dark embrace. Her skin would make the perfect camouflage.

Her breathing was irregular. She was very tired but she kept on running. And then, suddenly, she wasn't. Something was burning into her neck, something that was getting tighter and tighter. Her feet no longer touched the ground. They were kicking and flailing at the air, at the night, at the sound of laughter and cheers from a crowd. She couldn't see the people but she could hear them. She couldn't understand why they were so happy when she couldn't breathe.

Her eyes were tearing and felt as though they were going to explode out of her skull. She smelled smoke. A fire was burning somewhere. She felt the heat. Maybe it was more than one fire. She couldn't make it out when she was losing her breath—and then she was losing consciousness. Her legs no longer fought the darkness; now they were just swinging back and forth, brushing against the bark of the old oak tree.

Her eyes burst open. It was still dark, but the room was silent. The bed beneath her was soft, but something was wet. Her sheets were covered in her own sweat. Sierra sighed heavily, realizing that what she'd experienced was only a dream—but she was unable to relax. She was scared. Her dream felt real this time. More real than it had ever felt before.

She wanted to get up and wash her face or even get a glass of water, but she looked at the clock on the side of her bed and saw it was 4:00 a.m. In another hour she'd be forced to get up anyway, and she hated the idea of losing any more sleep than she already had. She'd been tired too many mornings lately. So she willed her mind to be still and her body to calm itself so that she could get back to sleep.

She closed her eyes and folded her hands, praying to God again for help, though she wasn't sure if He would hear or if He would even listen. A long time had gone by since last she'd prayed.

cɔ

Later that morning, Sierra found herself on the phone with her older sister, Irene.

"Hey, girl, what's up?"

"Nothing," Sierra replied. "I'm just getting ready to go meet with these clients." *And be just a little bored,* she added silently.

But her feelings didn't matter. Sierra relied on a common-sense mentality that kept her life and thoughts in rational order. She could always trust in logic when feelings made anything unclear.

"How did you sleep last night?" her sister queried in a worried voice.

Exhaling noisily, Sierra admitted, "Same as the last couple of nights this week."

"What are you going to do?"

"What can I do? I have to sleep, and every time I sleep, I dream. No matter what, the dreams keep coming, and talking about them won't make them go away. So what's the point of talking about them?"

Before Irene could answer, Sierra added, "Hey, let me get ready to go to this meeting."

She desperately wanted to get off the phone and out of this conversation.

The dreams were bad enough. She definitely didn't want to start her morning with a postmortem of the night before and the reminder that she was helpless to stop the nightmares.

Irene sighed. "Okay, talk to you later. I love you." She knew her sister well enough to know when she had taken the conversation as far as Sierra was willing to go.

"Love you too. Bye." Sierra disconnected the call, making a mental note as she did to call her sister later. She knew Irene would worry herself sick if she didn't.

Sierra was almost sorry that she'd told her sister about the dreams in the first place. She didn't want to be reminded of them. But she'd had a weak moment a couple of nights before and felt the need to tell someone about the nightmares that had been plaguing her all week. Now she knew her sister would harass her about it until she lied and told her that the dreams had stopped just to get her off of her back.

Although Irene was only four years older than Sierra, she had always had the uncanny ability to make Sierra feel like a child. Even now, she made her feel much younger than the twenty-eight-year-old woman she was.

Irene had a husband and three kids of her own. She was a stay-at-home mom, and she loved it. "You would think she had enough people to mother in her life," Sierra said aloud. She sighed and shrugged. *What are you going to do? That's Irene.*

Sierra had to direct her thoughts back to work. For her, being a real estate agent wasn't just about selling a house but rather selling a dream. As an agent, she needed to make her clients feel as though buying a house she was selling would be the culmination of all of their hopes. Conversely, when selling a house, she needed to make her owner clients feel that she would be persuasive enough to get the best deal for them, no matter what. In either situation, she had to be cheerful and confident. And that was the attitude she was determined to project today.

She picked up her purse and walked out her door to head to the property. The cold winter air hit her face as she left her condo and entered the parking lot of her building.

It was January, and winter was not yet ready to mellow out; on the contrary, it seemed determined to continue to roar like a lion. This particular morning, Sierra welcomed the sting of the wind on her cheeks. It was better than a slap to the face to revive her senses, wake her up, and help her to focus on the task at hand. It also propelled her even faster to her car, which, thankfully, was already running. She loved the trigger on her key chain that automatically started the Lexus.

She liked her career, too—especially because she made her own hours. She was glad to be doing work that offered her so much independence and was still monetarily advantageous.

She had spent a brief period after college working for an ad agency and hated it. She'd realized then that she wasn't made for nine-to-five hours and cubicles blocking the sunlight from her days. She didn't want to have to answer to an incompetent boss who took joy in coming to her desk every couple of hours to ask her questions to which, as the boss, he should already know the answers, and then watch him promptly take credit for all of her ideas.

My brilliant *ideas*, she amended, remembering that very unpleasant period in her life.

Anyway, that time was far behind her and she had more pressing issues to attend to right now, like showing a house. She began to do a mental check for the property she was about to show as she got in her car.

Right after she quit her job at the advertising agency, Sierra had happened upon real estate as a potential career. A friend of the family was a real estate agent and seemed to like it. Sierra told the woman she was interested and began to shadow her at work. She quickly learned the ropes, and soon thereafter, she took the necessary real estate courses and passed both the Wisconsin and national salesperson exams. The same brokerage that she'd shadowed under was registered on her initial license form, and she had been working under them ever since. Running her company through the brokerage allowed her the freedom to be her own person. The percentage of her commissions they took had always, until recently, seemed a small price to pay. Lately, though, she had begun to consider obtaining a brokerage license herself.

She took her work very seriously, which was reflected in the fact that most of her waking hours were spent on the phone talking to perspective clients, on the Internet looking at all kinds of listings, and in her car scouring the city and the surrounding area to keep up with where new communities were growing. All updates on property listings went directly to her phone and notified her with a distinctive ring. She even had an assistant/secretary, Stefani, who helped her stay on top of the mounting paperwork and clientele. Sierra ate, slept, and breathed real estate. And she loved her work—or at least she had convinced herself that she did for the last four years.

Stefani had e-mailed Sierra this morning with the details about the couple whom she was going to meet. They were an older couple looking for a summer house along Lake Michigan. They had been referred to Sierra by their daughter, who had recently bought a house through Sierra. Apparently, the daughter couldn't stop singing Sierra's praises to anyone who would listen, including her own parents.

Sierra was grateful for the referral, though the idea of a summer house struck her as both pretentious and enviable all at once. When this thought crossed her mind, she shook her head. Lately, she'd had contrasting opinions about just about everything. She was careful to keep these unsolicited ponderings to herself.

※

Sierra met the couple at the first house and proceeded to show them property after property along Milwaukee's lakefront. She looked at the columns on the houses, the beautiful bricks, the sprawling entryways, the landscaping, the neighborhoods, and the foamy white waves crashing along sandy beaches still dotted with remnants of icy snow and was suddenly angry but didn't understand why.

An overwhelming feeling of uneasiness began to plague

her. *What's happening to me?* she wondered. Then another unwanted thought arose. When was the last time she had done any volunteer or community work? *I can't be responsible for the whole world,* she told herself, and determined that she wouldn't be made to feel contrite about it. She then realized that she was arguing with herself. Again.

These internal scuffles had been happening with increasing frequency over the last couple of months. The skirmishes always ended in a draw, and she knew that today would be no different. So she put her mind back on the task at hand.

She looked around as she showed two more houses in the same neighborhood. She noticed the barren trees, which seemed burdened by the various snow masses weighing them down. Still other trees, those not as laden with precipitation, danced in the wind like electrified skeletons.

Sierra found half of her mind wandering like this for most of the day. Concentrating on real estate was hard when all she could think about was the disturbing dreams she'd been having. She was used to experiencing anxiety every once and a while and not being able to sleep. She'd even had nightmares before. But her usual fare were the kind of nightmares where you show up at some public function naked or you're falling from some tall building, or maybe even that your teeth are falling out. These new dreams were different. They felt so real that when she woke up she always felt a sense of terror—and relief. Sierra gently traced her fingers around her neck as a vague tightness briefly returned to her throat.

She couldn't understand what was going on and, more important, didn't know how she could make the dreams stop.

She had become too distracted lately. The lack of sleep was making her feel crazy. She had bags under her eyes and had been yawning for the past three hours. She didn't normally believe in drinking coffee every three hours, but for the last couple of weeks these constant caffeine boosts had become essential to her life. She really wanted to know what was going on inside her head. She needed to find out before her nights completely took over her days.

Chapter 2

*T*he sun was scorching hot, the kind of hot that made people think that the devil had decided to air out Hell. The wind was from the south and carried no oxygen. Sierra could feel sweat dripping from every pore in her body. Her mouth felt like sandpaper. She looked down at her hands, and all she saw were blisters and blood. Her hands were so sore and so weak that she was unable to bend her fingers. How did she get here? She looked all around her and all she could see for miles were fields of fluffy whiteness. She was in a cotton field.

All about her, people were steadily working. Everywhere she turned, she saw people working the field. They all looked tired. She heard some kind of humming all around her, but she couldn't make out what it was or where it was coming from. Children as young as six and men who looked as old as seventy were picking the cotton. She had a bale over her own shoulder, and her bale was definitely not as full as everyone else's.

Suddenly, she heard a loud crack. She felt the skin on her back open up, and a mixture of blood and sweat traveled down her spine like a river. The pain was excruciating. The

crack of the whip had been violent and quick. Sierra turned
and saw the menacing face of the overseer who had delivered
the harsh blow.

"You lazy nigger, your bag is 'bout empty compared to
everybody else's. Let this be a warning, and get to work."

Sierra heard the sound in the air again, like thunder, before she felt that whip again peel off her humanity. The river
of blood on her back split into tributaries as the final lick
came down. She stood frozen for a second and then started to
scream. Everyone in the field began to stare, and that's when
she heard it. She realized they weren't humming; they were
singing. She knew this song. "Steal away, steal way, Lord. I
ain't got long to stay here."

Sierra looked up and saw the kind eyes of an older
woman who had come close and was standing over her. The
woman was singing the song with the others as she looked
directly into Sierra's eyes, and a sudden peace coursed
through Sierra.

"I ain't got long to stay here."

Sierra hoped for her sake this was true.

Sierra looked in the mirror at her bloodshot eyes and down
at the eye drops in her hand. She hoped they would work,
because she knew she looked as if she had a hangover. That
wasn't the case, of course; it had just been another sleepless
night. Due to the nightmares, she couldn't get even two
hours of uninterrupted sleep. She'd been spending most of
her nights tossing and turning and hoping for peace.

Several more weeks had passed and the dreams persisted. She wasn't sure how much more she could take and still maintain her sanity.

The dream she'd had last night had confused her, and now it monopolized her thoughts. If she closed her eyes, she could still feel the lashes coming down on her back. That pain was real. She hadn't even had time to get angry or try to retaliate against the overseer. Everything had happened so quickly, and then she'd heard that song and received something from that woman—that woman who'd looked at Sierra as if she understood something Sierra didn't. The moment that had passed between them mystified and unnerved her even now.

She took in a calming breath and then slowly let it out. She put the drops in her eyes and gazed at herself in the mirror. "The show must go on," she said, giving herself one last look. She looked good, even with the bags; she was a good-looking woman. Her dark-brown skin was beautiful, blemish-free. The only mark on her face was a tiny scar right below her left eye. But her eyes were the main attraction on her face. They were big, hazel, and expressive.

Her mouth, her full lips, her round face, everything worked together to create a uniqueness that could never be manufactured. But she rarely gave her looks any thought beyond how she was projecting herself to the world. She was a professional and tried to convey that in her physical presentation. She worked really hard to be perfect in everything, hoping that if she achieved perfection, she would have happiness.

Sierra patted a strand of her short, dark brown hair back into place so her bob cut was as sleek as it was meant to be and then shrugged her shoulders. She turned from the mirror and walked out of the bathroom into the kitchen.

She was very thankful that she'd decided to buy coffee last night, because she desperately needed a boost right now. Actually, that was an understatement; she didn't need a boost, she needed a miracle.

As she began to make the coffee, she made a conscious effort to put last night's dream on the back burner. Today was a day full of things she needed to do, and obsessing about dreams wasn't on her list. That would have to wait.

The day was a gorgeous—and rare—sunny Saturday in early February. The sun had actually warmed the air to a very tolerable level. The weekend was finally here, and Sierra had a million things that she needed to do. She had some clients to show houses to early this morning, as she did on most Saturdays, and then she was supposed to meet her family for lunch. She even had a date set for later that night.

It had been a while since Sierra had agreed to go out with anyone, as she never really met anyone she liked and anyone she was interested in always turned out to be wrong in some way. She had always figured that when the right man came along, she would just somehow know. Unfortunately, that "knowing" feeling continued to elude her. Still, she remained hopeful.

She had to get going; time, she knew, waited for no man or woman. She took her coffee to go.

⁕

Sierra soldiered through another showing, this time in Mequon, a suburb of Milwaukee. She left the showing confident that she had convinced these last clients to buy—a fact that made her ecstatic, as the commission would be impressive. She jumped in her car and headed toward her parents' house, where she was sure that either comedy or mayhem would ensue.

"Either way, I'm ready," she said, out loud and encouragingly, to herself.

She knew her family was crazy—but no more than everybody else's, she assumed. By this point in her life she had created a coping mechanism to get through the crazy. She willed her mind to be prepared not to take offense to comments that were meant to be helpful, no matter how insanely inappropriate and hurtful they might be. And she, in turn, would try not to be judgmental and lecture her family on how they could and should handle their own issues.

She was still meditating on her mechanism when she pulled up in front of her parents' house, a two-story brick home that was originally built in the 1920s, like most of the houses in that area of Milwaukee. The block was near an area that had once been known for its stunning homes and immaculate landscaping but over the years had gone down in property value. Now, the neighborhood was experiencing new interest. Homes that had long been on the market with no bites were now being bought and renovated by natives of the city.

The revitalization here was something that warmed Sierra's heart as she got out of the car. Because it was February and Valentine's Day season, she spotted red and pink hearts decorating the front window as she walked up to the house. All the families in this neighborhood traditionally decorated their homes according to the holiday season. Her parents were no different.

As soon as she hit the door, she could smell the fried chicken. The open kitchen windows allowed that familiar scent to waft through the air to the front porch. She knew she would smell like chicken for the rest of the afternoon, but she was also convinced that the taste of that chicken as it hit her tongue would be totally worth it.

This house, always filled with enticing aromas and crowded with relatives, never changed. A cake or pie was always sitting on the table, and gospel or the blues was always pouring through the living room, telling stories of hope or despair. And, of course, there was always Pearl.

"Hey, baby," she said. "Come on in."

"Hey, Ma," Sierra said.

"What's been going on?"

Sierra's mom was very short, about five feet and one inch, but no one ever noticed that because her personality was so big. Although Sierra's dad had died almost ten years ago now, she could still remember her mother being the dominant force in their marriage.

Her dad had been a tall, dark, and quiet man who loved to work. He had worked for Harley-Davidson for thirty years. He'd started off on the factory floor and worked his way up to a managerial position. He had loved to have fun.

Pearl was thin, with the exception of her bust and waist. Her skin was like caramel and almost wrinkle-free, mocking her almost sixty years on this earth. But it was her mesmerizing smile and talkative, friendly nature that got most people to love her. Sierra's mother was known for getting people to open up and share their problems and secrets by using her soothing smile and the warmth that flowed through her being. That smile reached into her eyes and put everyone at ease. She had worked for the Public School System for over thirty-five years as an administrative assistant before she retired, and she'd never lost her ability to care for others—or to multitask.

Sierra realized her mother was still waiting for a response. "Nothing," she said, "just life."

"Well, that's something. Life is precious," her mother reminded her firmly.

"Mama, I know. I just meant nothing exciting is going on."

"Well, say that then, but don't say nothing's going on, because God can make it so that nothing really is going on." Pearl shook her head.

"Okay, Ma, I'm sorry." Even as Sierra apologized aloud, silently she thought, *And the foolishness begins.*

"What's up, ugly?"

Sierra's little brother, Ron, entered the kitchen in a crisp white T-shirt and dark blue jeans that hung just a bit low, making a mockery of the wide, black belt with the large silver buckle fitted around his waist. He held a thick brush in his hand and was brushing his light brown hair as though his life depended on the neatness of the waves on his head.

Sierra smiled in spite of herself. "Hey, little brother, what's up with you? Other than making me seasick with those waves."

Ron smiled and gave Sierra a nod, choosing to take her ribbing as a compliment.

But Pearl replied, "I'll tell you what's up with him, laying his lazy tail around my house doing nothing."

"Mama, please," Ron said.

He was a handsome young man. He had smooth, very light skin with a red undertone, and that had also hardly ever seen an imperfection in the twenty-two years since his birth. Ron, Irene, and Sierra could all thank their mom for their flawless complexions. Ron's hair was naturally wavy and light in color. When he was younger, people had often called him "Red" due to the color of his hair and bright skin tone.

Ron stood at six three and was that special kind of build of muscle and lean-without-ever-working-out that only comes with the metabolism of a twenty-something male. He was also unemployed and had dropped out of college a year previously. Since that time, he'd been living with their mother, "finding himself." And to say that Pearl and Ron were starting to get on each other's nerves was an understatement.

"Don't 'Mama, please' me. When you start paying some bills around here, then you can ask for me to get off your back. Until then I'm gonna be on you. You hear me!?" Sierra's mom turned and confronted her son as if she stood the same six feet he did. Pearl was usually mild mannered, but she had a temper that everyone, especially her children, knew not to be on the wrong side of.

"Yeah, I hear you. Can we eat?" Ron sighed with exasperation, but Sierra knew that "Life's too short to not live it relaxed" was his motto. He wasn't going to let a little nagging from his mother worry him too much. And besides, he knew just what to do to draw attention away from himself.

"Sierra looks thin, don't she, Mama?" he said in an innocent, concerned voice that belied the smirk he was giving his sister. This strategy worked every single time.

"She does look a little thin," Pearl said, concern written all over her face.

Sierra knew what was coming next, and she was pissed at her brother for drawing attention to her, because now she was in for an interrogation.

Sierra eyed her brother, pursed her lips, and gave him the finger behind her mother's back.

"You been eatin', baby?" Pearl asked.

Sierra sighed. "Yes, I've been eating. But I definitely wouldn't mind ending this conversation and getting some of the macaroni you made."

Ron, not intending to let the matter go, said, "When was the last time you had a meal?"

Sierra decided she'd had enough. "When was the last time you had a job, or even an interview? How about when was the last time you got a check that didn't have Mama's or Irene's name and address at the top of it?"

Ron lost his cool. "You know you think you're so smart, but don't nobody care that you got a job," he spat. "You got a job and no life. Oh no, I'm so jealous. I wish that I could work all the time and have no life beyond that." He pointed a finger at her. "I hope I never get to be like you!"

"F . . . you!" Sierra responded, holding back the curse, remembering just in time that her mother was in the room.

"All right, stop it," Pearl declared in a voice that demanded the argument be over. "That's enough. I don't want to hear y'all talk to each other like that. You guys are brother and sister. You should be loving each other."

Truth be told, there was never a question in Sierra's mind about whether or not she loved her brother; whether or not she liked him, however, remained to be seen. She apologized to her mother. Then, looking at the clock, she said, "Mom, I really have a full schedule today. I need to get going." She could feel herself taking her emotions inward, as she usually did—sometimes for other people's sake, but mostly really for herself. Being transparent was not in her comfort zone.

"You haven't even eaten anything," Pearl said, sounding really disappointed.

"I know," she said apologetically. "It's cool. Just make me a plate and I'll take it to go."

Now Ron jumped in. "You don't have to leave. I'm sorry."

Sierra looked at her brother. She could tell he really meant it. He liked to tease her, but he never wanted her to be really angry with him, and she could certainly hold a grudge.

He was usually sorry.

That's the problem, Sierra thought. *He is just too sorry.*

After her mother finished making her plate, Sierra kissed her on the cheek. "Love you," she said. "See you later."

"Bye," Ron said.

Sierra grunted in return.

She walked out to her car and placed the food on the passenger seat, willing the tears not to start. "Please, not now. You will not cry," she told herself. And just the way she had a million times before, she swallowed her sorrow and let it settle inside of her chest. When she finally felt that familiar knot, she knew she had succeeded. She smiled, satisfied, and started the engine.

Chapter 3

$\mathcal{A}$fter running around all day paying bills and shopping, Sierra was finally back home. She looked around her condo. She loved it here—loved every single inch. It was her sanctuary, and she had spent many hours placing pillows and rugs here and paintings and candles there so that the sights and sounds of her home would be as comforting as possible.

It was a two-bedroom, two-bathroom condo. She used the second bedroom as a guest room. Occasionally, her sister or brother or an out-of-town friend or cousin would stay the night, but mostly the room doubled as storage space.

The kitchen was custard yellow, and had the silver and black appliances and granite countertops that came standard with most of the condos in her building. The walls of the living room were a calming green, and the room was outfitted with a loveseat and sofa, both upholstered in a very plush red chenille. Vibrantly colored pillows were strategically placed on both pieces.

On her dark wood coffee table was an illuminated relaxation fountain that simulated a streaming brook with multicolored rocks throughout. The water in the fountain continuously flowed, recycling itself.

Two floral paintings shared the walls with family photos. One of the paintings was a beautifully abstract print of a red rose. The other was a popular print of a painting of white magnolia flowers. On the adjacent wall, a thirty-six-inch television was surrounded by an entertainment center. However, Sierra was most proud of her record player and the albums she had been collecting for years. Many of them she had gotten from her mom, sister, and older cousins; the rest she bought at various novelty music shops and online. She had everything from gospel to hip-hop to rock, and even a little country.

The floors of the condo were oak hardwood except in the bedroom; there, Sierra had installed cream-colored carpet, the softest she could find. The walls were a light blue, almost the color of the ocean. Floral paintings hung from the walls of the bedroom as well, prints from an impressionist painter known for capturing nature. And although the entire dwelling had a chill vibe, her bedroom was the most relaxing area in her space. The setup and color scheme made her think of the ocean and the beach. Every time she entered the room, she felt instantly relaxed and just wanted to lie down for hours.

Prior to the advent of her dreams, Sierra had loved coming home. Lately, though, she often wondered how she had gotten here—"here" being having a lovely home that she shared with no one and having a career that she had begun to question her reasons for pursuing, other than that it gave her the means to afford this condo, which was downtown, just off Water Street, and overlooked the Milwaukee River; her three-year-old Lexus; and having her hair and nails done weekly. These were all things that a couple of years ago had seemed vitally important. Lately, they made her feel like a fraud.

She remembered how, when she got her bachelor's degree in business and marketing, she'd thought that along with owning her own business, she was going to open a community center offering all kinds of extracurricular activities for kids, including self-esteem classes for young girls. She had spent a lot of time volunteering as a Big Sister in college and had loved it. The volunteer work had left an indelible mark on her.

She had also loved the art classes she had taken in college— painting, drawing, photography, she took to them all. As a child, she had loved to draw and had a natural talent for it, but had always kept the talent hidden. She would draw all kinds of things and then hide the drawings under her bed, never telling anyone about them. By the time she was in high school, she had stopped drawing completely. But something made her pursue it again in college.

Sierra smiled as she remembered the realization she'd had in college after volunteering and taking the art classes that she wanted to be an artist and spend her days working with youth, helping young people to see their full potential, and her nights painting the injustices of the world. None of that had seemed practical, however, so all of these thoughts remained in the back of her mind.

Now, sitting on the couch, she made a conscious decision that she would start painting again. She wanted that feeling of accomplishment that she got when she put paint to canvas and conceived of a new creation. Painting was a way to express herself—her true self—and maybe the lack of that expression was what had been hurting her lately. Her insides felt bulky, like that feeling one gets when one overeats.

She was carrying too much inside. She needed to relieve herself of some of her baggage. She curled up on the couch in her living room and watched the television watch her.

She had checked her voicemail when she got home from her errands and found a message from Dale, who was supposed to be her date for the evening. Apparently, he'd come down with some kind of sickness and wanted to reschedule.

Sierra was confused as to how she could have missed Dale's call; she didn't remember silencing her ringer—yet she must have. It was the only reasonable explanation. In any case, she didn't bother to call him back right away. If she was being honest with herself, she hadn't been really excited about the date from the start. He was one of her mom's friend's nephews, and the setup was the result of Pearl and her friend deciding to play matchmaker. According to the two of them, he was a physician who owned his own practice and came from a "good" family, whatever that meant. Pearl hadn't been able to honestly comment on Dale's looks because she had never met him.

I'll call him back later on, Sierra decided. Right now, she would much rather lie on her couch and silently stare at the television. Slowly, she relaxed her thoughts as she switched from channel to channel, and eventually she managed to zone out altogether.

Chapter 4

*A*re you awake? Dorothy, are you listening? We need to get ready. We're almost there."

"Who's Dorothy?" Sierra sleepily replied.

"Dorothy, are you all right? Open your eyes, honey. It's almost time to get off the bus."

Sierra's eyes flew open as she realized that she was no longer on her couch but on a bus with a group of people, all of whom looked at once scared, excited, and anxious.

"Where am I? Where are we going?"

The young woman's expression changed as deep frown lines began to wrinkle her forehead.

"Dorothy, we're on a bus, and we're almost at our stop. Don't you remember?"

Sierra looked out the window and watched the farmland, empty pastures, and dirt roads pass her by. She then started to take a good look at the woman staring at her as if she had two heads. The woman's hair was cut into a small, neat Afro, and she was dressed in a yellow cotton shirtwaist dress with an A-line skirt. Sierra looked down and noticed that she herself was wearing something similar, with the exception that her dress was black and white.

Sierra knew what was going on. She was dreaming. She also knew that just like all the dreams before, it would start with fear and end with violence. She began to feel a little hysterical. She wanted to scream, but the woman was already looking at her as if she was one straitjacket away from the nuthouse.

I need to try and wake myself up.

Sierra lowered her hand and began to pinch her thigh as hard as she could, hard enough that the pressure from her fingertips brought tears to her eyes, and then she began to chant in her head, *Wake up, wake up.* She closed her eyes and took a deep breath. She waited for the soothing smell of pumpkin spice that would indicate that she was back in her living room, surrounded by her scented candles—but all she could smell was the stench of too many bodies on a bus without air.

She kept waiting. Finally, her companion took her by the shoulders and shook her.

"Dorothy, you're really starting to scare me," she said. "Are you sick? Do you need some water? Please don't do this to me. You know I need you. You're the brave one."

Sierra could hear the panic in the woman's voice, and she wanted to reassure her, but she honestly didn't know what to do. She wanted to wake up before this bus got to its destination. She looked around the bus again and saw faces of varying ethnicities staring ahead and out of the windows in a daze. She grew curious. For now, she would see where this dream was going.

"What's your name again?" she asked the woman in the yellow dress.

The woman looked at her with that same confused look and took her hand. "Dorothy, I'm Mary. We've been best friends for all our lives. You know that. Now can you please pull it together? Because you're really scaring me."

"That's right, Mary," Sierra said. "I'm sorry. I guess I've been real tired, and when you woke me, I forgot who I was for a second. That's all."

Mary didn't look particularly convinced but seemed to decide to let the matter go for now. No doubt she would ask Dorothy about it again later on. Right now, it was more important that they were both prepared for the challenge that lay ahead.

"We're almost there. We need to start praying and make sure that we're prepared for spiritual warfare." Mary reached for Dorothy's hands and closed her eyes. Dorothy closed her eyes as well, and listened as Mary started to pray for their safety.

"Dear God, we come to you as humbly as we know how, just saying thank you, Jesus, for allowing us to get this far and to see another day. We just ask, dear Lord, as we embark on this journey, that you be with us, oh Lord. Lord God, protect us and keep us. Lord, you said that you would send your angels to keep us lest we dash our feet against a stone. Lord God, we ask that you do exactly that. And, Lord, let us feel the strength of the Holy Spirit inside our hearts, our minds, and our souls." Mary tightened her grip on Sierra's hands. "Lord, let us be warriors, but warriors of peace, Father. Lord, you said that faith the size of a mustard seed could move mountains, and Lord, I believe that. Keep us safe, oh God.

Keep us brave, and, Lord God, keep us in perfect peace. I love you, Father. Thank you, Jesus. In Jesus's name we pray. Amen, Amen, and Amen."

As Mary finished her prayer, Sierra could see that her eyelashes were moist from the tears that she didn't seem to realize were falling. Sierra's eyes, too, were wet with tears. She was moved by the prayer and realized that she recognized it as one similar to the kind her mother used to pray after her dad died and she'd had a bad day. Pearl would pray, and Sierra would close her eyes and listen. Sierra hadn't heard anything like it in a while.

She took a good look at Mary. She was of medium build, with rich, dark skin the color of a milk-chocolate bar, about the same as her own. Mary's eyes were slanted downward, as if in a frown. The irises were the color of brown quartz. Her fingernails were nubs, with the fingertip hanging over the nail. She was definitely a nail biter.

"We'll be at the station in ten minutes!" the bus driver called out.

Sierra felt queasy in the pit of her stomach. She was starting to understand what might take place when she got to this bus station.

This dream was different than the rest. Never had the dreams been this specific. In the past, the settings had always been some unknown plantation or anonymous forest. She'd never had a name in any of the other dreams. She'd never had a friend.

This is absurd. This is absolutely ridiculous, and I need to wake up right now. Please, somebody, come over, ring the doorbell, call me. Wake me.

But none of those things happened, and as the bus pulled into the station, she felt a little faint at the thought of what was to come. And as she felt her palms, moist with perspiration caused not just by the heat of the cramped bus but also by nerves, she realized that someone had her right hand in a death grip. It was Mary.

Mary looked straight ahead at nothing at all. Her profile was that of a warrior. No smile, no frown, just determination etched in the lines of her face.

The only indications of Mary's nervousness were the tiny beads of sweat that started at her hairline and rolled down her skin like condensation on a glass of ice-cold water and the grip she had on Sierra's hand. As Sierra watched Mary, she remembered that Mary had said that Dorothy, in fact, was the brave one. But right now, "Dorothy" felt nervous enough to pee in her pants and allow the itchy, warm feeling to distract her from what lay ahead.

She looked back again at Mary as the bus came to a stop. She realized that no matter what else happened in this dream, she would have to face the challenge outside of this bus. She pinched her thigh with her free hand one more time before relinquishing the hope that she could wake up from this dream before anything bad happened. But then another thought occurred to her: *I'm dreaming. This is my dream. Perhaps I can will myself to be in another place, a happy place.*

She concentrated on trying to change the location of the dream. She closed her eyes and thought of a tropical island. Nothing happened. The bus driver opened the doors, and she sighed.

She and Mary were with the first group of people to exit

the bus. There was no turning back now. As she stepped off the bus, she could smell the oppressive, thick air. It was stiflingly hot. The sun beat down on her skin like laser beams. She could feel her own hairline giving way to pools of sweat that trickled their way down her face.

The station looked abandoned. No passengers were waiting for their bus to arrive. No drivers were waiting in their own buses. There were no vagrants, no loiterers. There was no movement.

As all the other passengers filed out of the bus behind Sierra, she could feel her stomach drop to the floor, and once again that sick feeling of uneasiness took over.

It was only when the last group of passengers had left the bus that Sierra heard a loud stampede coming from both her left and her right. She couldn't see anything as the red earth of the station floor was kicked up, blocking her view.

She was confused. Were they going to be attacked by animals? All the passengers who had just exited the bus formed a tight ball around each other. Then the dust began to clear, and Sierra could see the herd of angry red and white faces looking at her. They held bricks, sticks, and two-by-fours. They were chanting something. She couldn't make out the words as the commotion around her began to take shape. Her fellow passengers were trying to crowd back onto the bus, but the doors were shut, and the driver had disappeared. They had nowhere to go, nowhere to hide. They would have to face the angry pack.

Sierra could finally make out what they were chanting. It was "Kill them all, kill them all."

Sierra winced as a tree fell down on top of her head. She

looked up; she didn't remember seeing any trees around the bus station. And then the second blow came raining down, and she realized it wasn't a tree but a fist. She fell to the ground as the pain gave way to a constant hammering inside her head. She put her hands over her face to block the blows, and to wipe away the sweat that was stinging her eyes.

More hits rained down. Sierra opened her eyes briefly and saw the blood covering her hands. She closed her eyes again and tried to protect her head with both her frail arms. Her attackers, seemingly tired of not being able to hit her in the face, began to kick her in the stomach and stomp on her legs and hands. Sierra's breath caught painfully; her lungs weren't getting enough air. She silently began to pray.

This was a dream, but the pain she was feeling was real.

Sierra and Mary had prayed for strength in spiritual warfare, and Sierra was now wondering whether they should have prayed for protection from physical warfare as well.

My ribs, my nose—are they broken? she wondered with dread.

The last violent kick broke something inside of her and she moved one of her hands down to her chest to try and hold that broken piece inside. As she moved her hand down her body, she realized that she was no longer holding Mary's hand.

Panic set in. Where was Mary? Sierra tried to open her eyes, but every time she tried she was met with a blinding, searing pain.

I have to try and find Mary, she thought, feeling a sudden protectiveness of the young woman, akin to what she would feel if she lost her sister. She needed to find her friend who had so much faith. She gathered herself together and prepared to take the pain when the light would once again deliver agony.

She could still hear the violent noises in the background. She could hear the sound of bones cracking and people crying out in torment. She could hear the roar of the angry crowd still yelling out obscenities, the hate coming down so swiftly and violently that she was convinced the words must be catching fire in the air. She could feel that angry heat, searing on her cheek. Sierra took a deep breath and opened her eyes.

Chapter 5

*S*ierra looked around her and realized that she was on the living room floor in her home. The blinding headache was still there. She put her hand to her face and felt a moistness around her nose. She wiped the liquid from her nose and confirmed that it was, in fact, blood. She tried to get up, but she felt as if she had been kicked in the ribs. And hadn't she? She had never heard of a dream that made your body sore.

Her phone lay beside her on the floor and she swiped the screen, unlocking it. Not only had she slept through the night but, according to the screen, she had slept through most of Sunday. It was five o'clock in the afternoon already. She had been asleep for almost eighteen hours.

Dang, she thought. She had missed church. Her intention had been to go this weekend. Since the dreams started, her desire to go to church had returned.

She slowly pulled herself up so that her back was against the couch. She looked out the window and observed the orange tinge in the sky that signaled day giving way to night. Darkness still came early.

Using the arm of the couch for support, Sierra slowly pulled herself to her feet and gradually made her way to the bathroom, her head tilted back to slow the drip of blood from her nose. She looked in the mirror and realized that she felt worse than she looked. The only physical remnant from her dream appeared to be the bloody nose that she was presently plugging up with tissue. Her face looked normal, bearing none of the telltale signs of having taken a severe beating.

Then she noticed a throbbing below her left eye. She observed no swelling, but she did see redness and tenderness around her tiny scar. Her ribs still throbbed and so did her head, but they bore no bruises, no bumps. Other than the bloody nose, there was no material evidence indicating that what she'd experienced was anything other than a dream—or, more accurately, a nightmare.

As she stood staring at her reflection in the mirror, she tried to make sense of it all. "I mean, I know that dreams usually have some deeper meaning, but what could these dreams— what does this dream—really mean?" she pondered out loud.

She checked her nose and realized that it was no longer actively bleeding. She pulled the tissue out.

She felt heavy and groggy, the repercussions of sleeping for long hours at a time, but she just couldn't bring herself to lie back down. She left the bathroom and went to the living room to hop on her laptop and do some research. As she re-entered the living room, she noticed something that had eluded her attention before: the light on her cell phone was blinking, indicating a waiting voicemail.

She unlocked her screen and accessed her messages. The

voicemail was from her mom, asking her to call when she got a chance.

Sierra sat down in her cozy loveseat, and stared at her computer screen. What, exactly, was she looking up?

She began to look up dreams on a search engine but found twelve thousand entries on her first query. She decided to narrow her search to dreams and changes in the physical body. She clicked on a couple of sites that had something to do with dreams manifesting themselves in the physical and quickly realized that these sites dealt mostly with sexual dreams and reactions.

"No, not what I'm looking for," she whispered.

She kept scrolling down until she got to a page dealing with sleepwalking. She began to read and realized that sleepwalking-related injuries could occur, especially if someone got out of bed and started to walk around.

I don't remember walking or running anywhere. Not that she would, though; according to the site, people didn't normally remember the episode in the morning. And she had awoken on the floor, after all. She'd just assumed that she'd fallen off the couch, but it was possible that she'd moved around her place and caused the bloody nose by running into the wall. *But wouldn't a blow like that wake me up?* She thought so, but she didn't really know.

Sierra recalled how in the past she had hardly remembered her dreams in the morning. These new dreams were different. Whenever she awoke, she could remember in vivid detail every single moment, just as clearly as if it were happening presently. It was as if someone was playing a movie reel inside her head.

A shiver ran down her spine at the memory of the last dream. And then she remembered a biography she'd read in high school that was reminiscent of her dream. A book about the Freedom Riders.

She typed the words into the keyboard, and a slew of websites about African American history came up. She clicked on the first site, and the write-up told her that the Freedom Riders were students and adults who rode buses into the South to test the desegregation laws that were passed by Congress.

She clicked through to another website and a picture of a bus on fire reminded her of a book she'd bought for an African American history class in college. She put her laptop on the table and got up slowly from the loveseat, careful not to cause her sore ribs more pain, and went into her second bedroom. The bookcase in this bedroom held all her books, old and new. She searched the shelves until she found her old textbook, and then she flipped to the table of contents. Yes, now she remembered: the Freedom Riders were in the chapter about the civil rights movement.

The journey had begun as an attempt to test the Supreme Court's decision that segregated seating of interstate bus and rail stations was unconstitutional. The Southern states at the time were still uncooperative. As they traveled through the south, the riders were met with intimidation and violence. As Sierra read on she noted, the violence and lack of protection for the riders and drivers were among the challenges that threatened to end the freedom rides. However, college students and other volunteers, continued the rides , refusing to let them end because of threats and violence. And so it went.

Young and old had risked their lives in order to ensure that laws were upheld and rights were given.

As Sierra read on, her admiration for the courage and passion of the individuals who had participated in the protest grew. But she still couldn't understand why she would have a dream about the riders, let alone experience it as if she was actually one of the protesters. It just didn't make sense.

She returned the book to the shelf and walked back to the living room, pondering what she'd just learned. The people who had participated in those rides were courageous. She didn't feel as though she was a particularly courageous person. Then Sierra remembered Mary from her dream—Mary, so full of faith. Sierra felt as if she really didn't have any of that, either.

She sank into her loveseat. *That's my real problem; I don't know who I am anymore. I've tried so hard to be successful, but am I? I'm almost thirty years old, and still I have absolutely no idea what would truly make me happy.*

"What have I been doing with my life?" When she asked herself the question aloud, she felt a shiver run through her body.

As she allowed her inner monologue to vent, she began to feel overwhelmed and her heart started to beat out of rhythm, faster and faster. Breathing was becoming difficult. She was having a panic attack.

She hadn't had one since she was in college. But since she had been having these dreams for the last couple of months, she had started to feel her body responding to the stress.

She let herself float off the loveseat and onto the floor. She grabbed her chest, and as she leaned over, trying to calm her breathing, she decided to pray again. She was still unsure if God was listening, but more and more she felt compelled to try. She had gotten it into her head that maybe God was angry with her—as angry as she had been with Him once upon a time. This was one the few times as an adult that she had felt like she really needed Him, and in her mind she thought He might feel used. She certainly would.

"God, if you're listening, I want you to know that I need you. I know that I haven't talked to you in a while, but I need you. I need you to make this stop. Please, please. Make it stop. In Jesus's name. Amen."

Her hand was still over her heart, as if that could control the feeling of her heart coming out of her chest. She willed her breathing to slow, and as she did, she realized that she was actually extremely tired. She couldn't believe it; she had literally slept all day, after all. But she felt exhausted.

The heart palpations were starting to slow, so she was able to make it to her feet and across the living room to her bedroom. Her four-poster sleigh bed looked like an oasis in the desert. She dropped down on the bed and curled into the fetal position. Her whole body was shaking like a leaf from her nerves.

After about ten minutes of staring at the walls that were meant to bring her tranquility, Sierra's shaking stopped, her breathing became regulated, and her eyes grew heavy. After about only a two-and-a-half-hour break, sleep had taken her again.

Chapter 6

Sierra opened her eyes and found that she was staring at the floor. The floor was grimy and sticky and smelled of urine. She could feel sweat coming from every pore of her body. She looked around her and had to shut her eyes pretty quickly because she felt so woozy.

She struggled to open her eyes again, and this time she succeeded. Her pupils dilated as the only source of light in the room, the moonlight, came in through the bars of the window above her head. She looked directly ahead, and her gaze was met with the parallel bars of a jail cell.

She adjusted her body so that her back was all the way up against the wall and scanned her surroundings. At least ten or eleven other women were in the cell with her. Their collective body heat and the heat of the night air coming in through the window combined to make the cell unbearably humid. Most of the women she recognized from the bus, but one or two she didn't remember seeing before. Her head still felt heavy, but the explosion of pain that she'd felt on first opening her eyes had already dulled to a low throbbing.

Sierra knew she was back in her dreams. This time,

though, she didn't panic. She knew that at any moment she could wake up, and she wanted to try and find some understanding as to why she was having this dream before that happened. In doing so, she hoped to obtain closure and put an end to the dreams, period.

The first order of business was to find her friend. She lost Mary in the commotion outside of the bus. Was she here in the cell? Sierra looked all around, but none of the faces belonged to her friend.

"Do you know where we are?" she asked a young woman to her right who seemed particularly frightened.

"All I know is that they brought us to this place in a paddy wagon after the mob got tired of beating on us," the girl replied.

"What charge are they holding us on?"

The girl had no clue, but the woman on the other side of her said, "We're being held for instigating a riot, resisting arrest, and being Negroes."

Sierra looked around for her friend again, this time calling into the darkness of the overcrowded cell, "Mary, Mary, are you here?"

"Dorothy?" a weak voice called from the farthest end of the cell from where Sierra was sitting. "I'm here."

Moving carefully to avoid stepping on the sleeping bodies strewn across the floor, Sierra hurried to the other end of the jail cell to check on her friend. As she picked her way through the crowd, she observed women with bloody gashes on the sides of their heads, and others whose dresses were ripped so badly that their underwear was visible.

When she finally reached Mary, she put a hand under her

friend's chin and lifted her face so that she could see her more clearly. Her face was wet with perspiration and tears, and her right eye was puffy and closed. The circumference of the eye was black and blue. The other eye looked at her friend with sadness and pain.

Sierra hugged Mary as tightly as she could with her bruised ribs and asked her, "Are you okay?"

"I'll be all right," Mary said. "How about you?"

Until that very moment it hadn't even occurred to Sierra to check herself for injuries again. When she was in her own living room, she had checked herself and found no real damage. Now, however, she put a hand to her head and realized that she had a bloody wound near her hairline the size of a small child's hand. She also noticed discomfort and throbbing under her left eye. Her hand drifted down her face under her eye and felt a small, fresh wound that had made its home under her left eye, in the same place where her old scar presided. And then that thumping came back inside of her head as well, calling into memory the many aggressive blows that she had taken.

"I'll be fine too," she finally replied, although she wasn't all the way convinced that she didn't have a slight concussion. She met Mary's eyes again. "Where are we and how did we get in here?"

Mary replied, "We are in the county jail. I saw the sign when they brought us in. That's all I really remember. Everything else is just a blur."

"What do you think they'll do with us?"

"I don't know."

A guard came by the cell and rapped his stick against the

confining bars. "All right," he said. "Looks like you all will be here for a while, so I would suggest you get comfortable."

Someone near the front of the cell spoke up. "Sir, some people in here are hurt. Their wounds need tending."

"I don't see no people, only animals," the jailer said.

"Well, sir, even animals get to see a doctor when they're hurt," the brave woman answered.

"You think you hurt now, you just keep on talking and making trouble and see don't I show you what hurt is," the jailer yelled, his words full of malice.

The woman speaking looked down at the wound on her shoulder and kept her silence.

Probably saving her energy, Sierra thought. *Lord knows she'll need it.*

A younger woman with a bloodstain on her flowered dress piped up. "When can we have a phone call?" she demanded. "That's our right."

"You ugly little nigger," the jailer said, leaning forward. "You ain't got no rights. The sooner you understand that, the better off you'll be."

Without waiting for a response, he abruptly walked off, leaving the women in the dark. As they lay on the floor, broken and bruised, stomachs growling, an easy silence settled in. And then whispers began to pervade the air. Women who were lying down rose to their knees to pray. Hands folded, heads bowed, they chanted, "Jesus," over and over again.

Soon, Sierra and Mary were on their hands and knees as well, thanking the Lord for their lives and asking that He continue to give them strength and courage. Cries of joy and sorrow began to fill the air as a sweet spirit moved around the jail cell. One by one, the women began to shout in the way of the old church while a feeling of uncontrollable joy took them over.

Sierra found that she wasn't immune to the spirit; in fact, as the praying continued, she began to feel whole. She felt a tingling sensation in her fingers and toes as her hands went up in the air, and as tears flowed down her now warm cheeks.

"Jesus, thank you Jesus." Over and over again, she kept repeating these words. And then she began to exclaim, "I love you, I love you, I love you!" until her whole body felt as if it were floating through the air.

This went on and on for what felt like hours. At some point, the prayer was broken by a woman starting to sing, "Leaning on the Everlasting Arms."

Leaning,

Leaning,

Safe and secure from all alarm …

Soon, all the other woman joined in.

Leaning,

Leaning,

Leaning on the Everlasting Arms …

Their outcry seemed to come from the depths of anguished souls, and when the song ended, all that could be heard in the air was heavy sobs.

"Father God," the women said. "Thank you, Jesus."

Sierra felt her body begin to sway to and fro, and her eyelids felt familiarly heavy. She was once again exhausted, but this time she was filled with a peace that she hadn't experienced before. She let her eyes drop closed, and she gave in to the darkness around her.

Chapter 7

⁓ℓℓℓ⁓

*W*hen Sierra again opened her eyes, she was lying in her bed. Her body was worn out and she had a severe headache. She rose slowly, lest she upset her head again. She ran her hands through her hair, stretched, and yawned. Once she had oriented herself, she slowly made her way to the bathroom and splashed water on her face. She opened the medicine cabinet and reached for the bottle of ibuprofen. After popping the pills in her mouth, she cupped her hands and washed the medicine down with tap water.

She wondered how long she'd been gone this time. As she walked into the living room, she saw the blinking light on her phone indicating she had a voicemail. She played the first message: "It's Mom. I was just calling to see how you were doing. Love you. Give me a call when you get this message. Bye."

The next message was from her sister: "Hey, why aren't you answering either one of your phones? Call me."

The last message was from Stefani: "Hi, Sierra, I need to know that everything is okay. You had two showings you were supposed to do today, and I got complaints from the clients that you never showed. I'm wondering what's up. Give me a call. At least let me know that you're okay, and tell me what I should say to the clients."

Sierra began to panic. She couldn't believe she had blown off two showings. She was always on her game; she never missed a beat. *This is bad. This is really bad.* When she looked at the date on her cell phone, she realized that it was Tuesday. The showings Stefani was talking about had been scheduled for Monday. She had slept for over two days. How was that even possible?

She quickly found the information for the two clients and called them. One had already moved on to another real estate agent, but Sierra got the other one to agree to a showing that day after explaining she'd had a serious family problem.

As soon as she hung up the phone, Sierra got in the shower. Twenty minutes later, she was dressed in a black, boot-cut cotton pantsuit and white camisole and heading out the door.

She knew she was avoiding the fact that she had a very real problem on her hands with the dreams. She needed to figure out what to do about it. *But first I have to show this house,* she told herself. *I have to eat, right?*

Even as this thought came to her, a corresponding growl rumbled in her stomach, reminding her that sleeping for two days also meant not eating for two days. She promised herself she would pick up something before the showing.

The house she hoped to sell was a beautiful red brick residence in Brown Deer, another suburb of Milwaukee. The potential buyer, Steve Thomas, was a teacher with the Brown Deer public school system. He was thirty-three years old and a Milwaukee native. This would be his first time buying a home.

When Sierra met him on the sidewalk outside of the house, she looked up to speak to him and noticed how tall and handsome he was. But what really struck her were his gentle brown eyes. She wondered why she hadn't noticed them before.

Before she could go too far off on that tangent, she gave herself a mental slap.

As they entered the home, Steve shared, "I'm still not sure what I'm looking for in a house. But I think I'll know it when I see it."

Sierra wondered how, if he was a teacher, he was able to get off and meet her to see this house by two o'clock on a weekday. But she also knew it was none of her business. He was here and that was all she should really care about.

"Even buyers who think they know exactly what they want say the same thing in the end. Something about the house spoke to them. They knew it was the one when they saw it. I have no doubt you'll know too."

Sierra gave him a brief history and tour of the residence and then allowed Steve to explore on his own, as was his wish. She took the opportunity to have a little break herself. As Steve investigated the living room area, she headed toward the kitchen.

The kitchen was equipped with shiny new stainless steel appliances and a new coat of white paint, leaving the next owners to make up their own minds about what color they wanted to add to the walls. Sierra took a quick look around at the hardwood floor and granite countertops, assuring herself that nothing was out of place. Then she made her way to the sliding glass door at the back of the kitchen and gazed out at the spacious backyard.

A crabapple tree stood right in the middle of the yard's grassy, open space. This was definitely a family home. Plenty of opportunity remained for all kinds of landscaping or maybe even a swing set or pool. The possibilities were endless.

Sierra continued to stare, picturing children playing, laughing, and loving life in the inviting backyard. The thought brought a wistful smile to her face; she wondered about having children of her own. A yawn caught her by surprise, wiping away the smile, and she marveled at the fact that she had the audacity to be tired after having slept for the last two days. She knew that she would have to see a doctor in the near future; her sleeping issues were getting way out of control, and it was making her more irritable than normal.

A hand landed on her shoulder and she almost jumped out of her skin. "Oh!" she whispered, startled.

"Whoa, hey, relax," Steve said. "I didn't mean to scare you."

Sierra at first frowned in agitation and then remembered herself and relaxed. "I'm sorry, Mr. Thomas. You didn't scare me. I was just a little startled."

"Oh, well, whatever it was, I'm sorry—and please, call me Steve."

Sierra smiled and nodded her head slightly in acquiescence. "Okay, Steve. What do you think of the house?"

"I think I like it."

Sierra smiled. "Great. That's good news!" If she could wrap up this sale soon, she would be very happy.

"Yeah, I like it. And it's definitely one of the best ones that I've seen—but I'm still not sure," Steve said.

Her hopes dampened, Sierra sighed inwardly and put on her most confident smile. "Well, you don't want to wait too long, because a lot of people are interested in this property, and I would really hate for you to miss out on this great opportunity."

Steve smiled a knowing smile. He looked at Sierra as if he understood everything about her. "I'll be sure to keep that in mind while I'm thinking about it," he said.

Sierra didn't want to push too hard. "I have other properties that may suit your needs if you want to continue the search . . ."

"No," Steve said. "I want to think about this property before moving on to another one." He looked out at the backyard. "There's something special about this place."

After going over the square footage of the house and some of the extra features, including a finished basement and fireplace, Sierra knew it was time to wrap things up. "Well, have you seen enough for today?" she asked.

"Yes, I think I have," Steve said with a smile.

Sierra ushered him out of the house, pausing only to lock up behind her. "Well, thank you for coming to meet me on such short notice," she said, "and if you make up your mind or have any other questions, concerns, or requests, you have my number."

Steve shook her hand. "Yes, I have your number—and if I have any questions, I'll be sure to call you."

He didn't let go of Sierra's hand right away, and she could feel a sensation almost like an electric current go through their united hands, connecting them. She looked into his eyes and could see that he felt it too. As politely as she could, she dropped his hand, and without another word, she walked to her car.

⁓

Steve stood in the same spot outside of his own car for a full minute, still staring at the spot Sierra had just occupied even after she drove away. He felt as if he were frozen in place. His brain refused to let him do anything else for the moment.

When his mind decided to come back, he realized that he was able to open up his car door and get in—but he was still totally confused as to what had just happened. He was attracted to his agent, for sure. She was an extremely beautiful woman, so that wasn't unusual. What he did find perplexing, however, was how nervous and on edge she seemed. When he first met her, she had been very efficient and matter of fact, extremely confident in her abilities. Yet lately, she hadn't even called to check up on him. He'd purposely taken a half day yesterday to meet her at this location to see this house. When she hadn't shown up, he'd been more worried than angry—also perplexing—and then when she'd called to schedule this appointment, he'd agreed and taken off from school early, claiming an emergency, which he never did.

It confused him that he was still unsure of the reasoning behind his actions. Sure, he wanted to buy a house, but his possibilities for real estate agents were almost endless. And yet he didn't want anyone but Sierra. She had been agitated today, and he'd seen a tiredness in her eyes. For some reason, all of that tiredness and agitation was drawing him in like a moth to a flame. When he'd touched her shoulder in the kitchen, he'd had to stop himself from massaging her shoulders and trying to relieve some of the tension he felt there. It was a good thing he hadn't tried; she'd moved away from him so fast, she obviously wouldn't have welcomed his touch.

And then, just now as he shook her hand, he had felt an attraction between them—he'd felt it from his fingers to his toes. He'd looked at her stiff stance as she got in her car and realized that he would have to go slow. She didn't look ready to accept anything from anybody, least of all him. Would she even admit to herself that they had an attraction? *Probably not*, he thought as he started his car. He didn't know whether she was dating anyone. He hadn't noticed a ring, though, so he remained encouraged.

Sierra drove off as quickly as she could. She didn't quite know what just happened. She'd definitely felt some kind of attraction to Steve when their hands touched—but there was absolutely no way she could handle something like that right now. She just had too much going on. Besides, Steve was a client, and fraternizing was a personal "no-no" for her.

She sighed. It was just as well; it probably wouldn't have worked out anyway. She put her foot on the gas and focused her thoughts on the road ahead.

Chapter 8

"And what did the doctor say?" Irene inquired.

It was Friday. The week had flown by in a blur of house showings, phone calls, and listings. But somewhere in the midst of all that activity, Sierra had been able to get in touch with her primary care physician and ask him about her tiredness, her dreams, and her long bouts of slumber. She had gone to see him on Thursday and was now being questioned by Irene.

"Well? I'm waiting," Irene prodded.

Sierra groaned, realizing that nothing but the entire story would do for her sister.

And so she began. "He asked me a lot of questions about my sleeping patterns at first. When I told him that I thought I'd slept for three days straight this last week, he had a hard time believing me."

"I can understand why."

"When I told him about the nature of the dreams, he became concerned about points of stress that might be affecting my dreams. He asked me if my job is stressful, which to me was an idiotic question, because whose job isn't?" A bit chagrined, Sierra realized she might have actually told the doctor that his questions were idiotic.

"I'm guessing you let him know what you thought of his questions," Irene said dryly.

"He didn't seem to take offense," Sierra said. "He just told me that stress can definitely affect sleep patterns, and that sleep deprivation has been known to cause irritability, hallucinations, and of course tiredness. He also said that people who are depressed have prolonged sleeping habits and some of the same symptoms I described to him. After his physical examination, he found nothing out of the ordinary, and he suggested that it might be good for me to see a mental health specialist. He suggested a Dr. Elisabeth Cayden."

"So, the doctor thinks you're crazy?"

"No, the doctor doesn't think I'm crazy," Sierra shot back, unable to keep the irritation out of her voice. "He's merely suggesting that my problem is a mental rather than a physical one, and that talking to a professional about it might not be a bad idea."

"Are you going to?" Irene asked.

"I don't know yet," Sierra replied truthfully. "I haven't had any more dreams all week that I can remember. Maybe the dreams and the sleeping were my mind and body reacting to stress, and now that I've addressed taking care of myself, it will all go away."

"Well, I hope you're right," Irene said. "I've been really worried about you, especially when you sleep like that and can't even hear your phone ringing. Maybe you need to take a vacation and kind of get away for a while."

The idea seemed like a good one. "I'll give it some serious

thought," Sierra said. "As I said, I haven't had any dreams all week, so maybe that ship has sailed and I can get back to normal."

"I hope you're right," Irene repeated, still sounding worried.

Sierra also hoped that she was right. The dreams disturbed her well-being, not to mention interrupted her ability to function properly in her life. Now that they'd stopped toward the end of this week, she hoped that everything would return to normal.

Chapter 9

"The time has come for action. The time has come for change."

Boisterous clapping and amens filled the packed church.

Sierra was no longer surprised at opening her eyes and being in an unfamiliar place. She knew she was dreaming, and she was becoming an old hand at adjusting. After a quick scan of the crowd, she fixed her eyes back on the pulpit, like everyone else in the building.

"We have tried to patiently wait for them to give us our rights, to one day wake up and realize the error of their ways and come to the table of brotherhood with love and fellowship," the speaker continued. "But it seems that they will need a push in the right direction. And I don't know about you tonight, but I'm ready to give them that push."

More applause rained from the crowded pews of the sanctuary. In looking around, Sierra could see that the entire church was filled; people spilled into the hallways beyond the main hall, and even down the stairs that led to the outside of the building. Tonight was definitely standing room only.

Five ministers stood in the pulpit behind the current speaker, nodding their heads and giving their approval. The heat was once again stifling. Sierra was unsure whether the air conditioner was incapacitated or nonexistent. Regardless, no one but her appeared to notice. The single-mindedness in the atmosphere could not be denied. The excitement was electric and palpable.

To Sierra's left was Mary, who seemed completely recovered from her ordeal in jail. Sierra took a look at her own hands and gingerly brushed her scalp, face, and forehead, confirming that she too was healed. Apparently they had moved on from the wounds and violence of the last two dreams. Their outfits, however, were similar to those they had worn in the last dream. They wore shirtwaist dresses with A-line skirts that reached just past their knees. The only difference between their dresses was their color: Sierra wore black and Mary wore white.

Sierra felt a sense of community and togetherness in this church that she had never experienced in her whole life. Living in this time was dangerous and constrictive, yes—but despite the danger and injustice, everyone in the room seemed to be sure of their purpose, and they were working toward a common goal.

Together, the confusion Sierra felt at being back in this dream again and the powerful words of the speaker stirred her emotions. She felt light-headed in the boiling room.

She sat down, though everyone else remained standing, took a church fan from the back of the pew in front of her, and began to fan her face, hoping that the feeling of faintness would pass. She felt a gust of air to her left and looked up: Mary was holding another fan and fanning away, her face full of concern.

Mary sat down on the pew next to Sierra and got close to her ear. "Are you all right?"

"I'm all right," Sierra said. She gave Mary a smile to reassure her. She got back on her feet and joined the crowd in listening to the remainder of the speech.

"We started this boycott because enough was enough. We started this boycott because it is imperative that we finally take a firm stand against injustice. And believe me when I tell you that it is working. Believe me when I tell you that they are confused now. They never imagined that we could come together and stay focused for such a long period of time. They never imagined that our mothers and sisters and grandmothers and wives would be willing to walk so far, and so long. They never imagined that they would be willing to lose their jobs and withstand threats on their lives as a sacrifice to their future. And they never imagined that we would continue, just as we are continuing, until our demands are met and we're able to ride buses that are integrated from the front to the back. We will not stop until this is accomplished."

The audience responded to the hope and energy of the speech with uproarious cheers. They waved their hands in the air and slapped their palms in agreement with the speaker's call to action.

"Repeat after me," the speaker commanded. "The time has come."

"The time has come," the entire congregation echoed.

"The time has come."

"The time has come."

"The time has come."

Sierra felt tears flowing down her cheeks as she chanted along with everyone else.

The chanting continued for timeless minutes before finally dissolving into a chorus of another hymn.

Everyone joined hands and rocked with the rhythm of the song.

And the song went on and on.

Finally, the first speaker left the microphone, and another speaker stepped up to give out information about where pickups for the car pools would be for those who were planning to help with the boycott. "If any other volunteers would like to be drivers for the coming week," he said, "please come to the front of the sanctuary after benediction." He then said a prayer and dismissed the meeting.

Hugs and greetings broke out all over the sanctuary, with people talking to everyone they knew, as well as those they didn't.

Mary couldn't stop talking as she exited out of the pew before Sierra. "Aren't you excited? This is so exciting! It's working. Our plan is actually working. You know, I believe that the more threats that come our way and the more the city tries to intimidate us, the closer we are to breaking them. I mean, it's been how many days? Fifty or so. And no one, I mean no one, not one Negro, has gotten on a city bus. This is it. This is the movement. This is what we've been living for."

By now, Sierra had figured out that they were a part of a long-standing bus boycott to integrate city buses, and she remembered the admiration she'd felt for the people involved when she first learned about these efforts as a child. Now, somehow, through this dream, she was getting to take part, at least a little bit, in this important historical moment. The feeling was beyond anything that she could have ever imagined.

She tried to come up with a response to Mary's enthusiasm, but couldn't adequately communicate the rush of emotion she was experiencing. She settled for, "Yeah, this is all really overwhelming."

Mary began to usher Sierra through the crowd to the doors outside, stopping to say hi to different people along the way. The greetings were geared toward Sierra—or rather, Dorothy—as well, and Sierra tried to respond appropriately to everyone who addressed her.

Eventually, the two women made their way out to the hall. By that time the crowd on the stairs had dispersed, so they had no trouble making it to the sidewalk. When they did, Mary began to walk in a determined direction down the street—and Sierra, for lack of anything else to do, followed.

Mary was so full of excitement that she hardly seemed to notice how quiet "Dorothy" was, and she chattered on as they walked.

Sierra took note of the houses they passed, which all looked the same: modest, one-story homes with very well-kept yards.

They crossed the street and entered a commercial stretch. Lining the streets were storefronts that practically hugged each other in their closeness. The first was the local drugstore, marked with white letters and a pill bottle above its door. Directly to the left of the drugstore was a small grocer—who, according to the name written on his front window, was named Bill. Next to Bill was a butcher whose windows were darkened, though the shadow of meat encased in glass counters could be seen through the window.

Sierra took in the community and made a mental note that everything people would generally need was in walking distance of their homes. She breathed in the air and noticed that even here in the city—and that's what this place looked like, with its paved streets and streetlights—she could still smell the freshness of the country air and see fireflies dancing in the twilight. She looked up and could readily see the starry sky. Their surroundings were very . . . relaxing. Sierra laughed at herself for thinking such a thought at a time like this.

Such is the nature of dreams, she thought. *I'm totally relaxed in one moment and then taken to the height of anxiety and fear in another.*

"Dorothy, what you smiling about?" Mary asked in a bemused voice.

Sierra snapped out of her reverie and decided to be honest about her feelings. "I guess I'm just at peace, Mary. I feel content right now."

"I feel peace too," Mary said. "I feel like right now, at this very moment, we're at the point of something big. I feel that we're a part of something bigger than us. This is our purpose. In this moment, I feel I'm doing what I was put on this earth to do, and that does make me feel sure and content."

Sierra hadn't expected that kind of response, but she could understand how Mary was feeling. She'd felt it the moment she opened her eyes in the church. She'd felt it in everyone around her at the meeting. She could feel it inside of herself as Dorothy. It felt wonderful. She was living in the moment.

Mary stopped in front of a one-story that looked similar to all the houses they had passed. The house was old but sturdy, with four wooden steps that led to a wooden-planked porch. The black shingles on the façade blended into the night, but even so the house was oddly nonthreatening. The window facing the street emanated an orange and yellow light that created a light show on the well-kept lawn, and as Sierra peered at the glow, laughter sounded from inside the house.

She followed Mary as she walked up to the door. Mary knocked, and two minutes later the door was opened by a tall woman with skin the color of butterscotch and the kindest eyes Sierra had ever seen. She wore a housedress that was red with white lilies all over it, and a white apron spotted with stains here and there in a pattern that almost looked designed. She used the bottom of the apron now to wipe her hands as she spoke.

"Hey, baby, y'all back, hunh?" the woman addressed the young women.

"Yes, ma'am, Miss Patty, we are," Mary answered for both of them.

"Well, y'all come on in. I expect you're probably hungry by now. Why don't y'all come in the kitchen and grab a plate." Miss Patty held the door open for the two women and waited until they entered before shutting it behind them.

Sierra found herself in a living room full of people. They were all talking and laughing together. It wasn't a big room at all, and it was crowded. A couch stood to one side of the space, and a dining room table and chairs lined the other side of the room. Those who weren't sitting on the couch holding a plate and eating were at the dining table. The floors were hardwood and well worn.

The walls were covered with pictures, but Sierra didn't have time to inspect them—Miss Patty walked straight through the living room and toward the kitchen, and beckoned for Sierra and Mary to follow.

The smell captured Sierra before she even got to the kitchen. The air smelled of fried fish—an aroma that reminded Sierra of her mother's house. Suddenly, she missed her mother's cooking.

Miss Patty was already serving up ample helpings of the fish onto two plates and asking for details about the meeting at the church. Mary was only too happy to provide the particulars for her.

Surprisingly, one chair at the quaint, round, dark-wood table in the kitchen remained free, despite the fact that the kitchen was almost as crowded as the living room, and Miss Patty insisted that Sierra sit there. So she sat, ate, and eavesdropped on the other conversations around her.

Everyone was abuzz about the boycott—how well it was going, and how long it might take before the city would relent and allow integrated seating on the bus. Some thought the change would take a month, while others thought that perhaps the decision might be made within the week. No one seemed to feel awkward with Sierra sitting there; just as at the church, they all seemed to know her.

Miss Patty's food was absolutely delicious. Sierra marveled that she was so comfortable and everything felt so familiar, even though this place and these people were actually all new to her. She sat back and played the part of observer, taking in the excited atmosphere of bonding and togetherness.

This is so nice, she thought—and once again she was overwhelmed by the feeling of being a part of something important and bigger than herself. Once again, she felt compelled to confront herself about what she was doing with her real life. The heavy feeling that she sometimes felt around her heart when she was awake was returning to her now in her dream state.

Suddenly, a hand was on her shoulder, squeezing gently, and a male voice as charming as it was warm asked, "What's wrong, sweetheart?"

Sierra jumped a little at the sound of the deep, melodious voice so close to her ear, and she turned toward the speaker. There, standing behind her, was someone who had to be the best-looking man she had ever seen in her life. She was startled enough to actually come out of the chair that she was occupying before seating herself slowly again, utterly chagrined at her reaction.

The stranger stood looking down at her, smiling as if she were the cure to all his illnesses. That was the last coherent thought that she was able to muster up before big hands gently took hold of her face. In real life, a strange man who approached her in such a familiar manner would get a swift slap. Oddly, in this dream, such a reaction didn't even cross her mind; she felt too relaxed to do anything at all, though she couldn't tell if the dream or this man was the source of her feeling of calm.

At any rate, Sierra didn't get a chance to ask any questions or even answer the mesmerizing man's question before he came in for a kiss that she was sure was meant to be comforting but instead rattled her equilibrium and made her knees go weak.

The man slowly released her and looked into her eyes, still holding her. Sierra couldn't manage to say a single word.

"Dorothy, hey Dorothy!"

Someone was yelling her name from across the room. Sierra turned toward the sound, but no one was there. Then Miss Patty, Mary, and all the people in the kitchen were gone. As Sierra turned her head back around, she saw that the man was gone as well, and she was standing in the middle of an empty kitchen. There was no laughter, no food, no people, and no conversation—and then there was no light.

Chapter 10

$\mathcal{I}$t was the start of another week and a new month, March, though the weather outside still didn't want to quite recognize that spring should be in the air. Sierra had gone a whole week without any dreams before having the one about the church meeting over the weekend. Unlike with the dreams that had preceded it, however, she had slept only through the night; the next morning, she woke up at a normal time. The dream was also different in that she experienced no violence or fear. In fact, she had found it inspiring, and quite enjoyable. Even now, she thought about the kiss that ended the last dream and felt a tingle of excitement.

Nevertheless, she was kind of glad that she had already made the appointment to see Dr. Cayden on Monday. Today was the first day of the work week, and she was hoping for some answers and a fresh start.

Dr. Cayden was a petite woman with her hair in a bun and small, dark-rimmed glasses decorating her slanted green eyes. She didn't say anything when Sierra walked through the door.

"So, how do I do this?" Sierra asked after a few moments of standing there in silence. "I mean, what am I supposed to do?"

Dr. Cayden sat in a plush black chair with a high, stiff

back and swivel on the bottom that Sierra would have loved as a kid. She would have pushed her feet up against the floor and spun the chair round and round until she was so dizzy she wanted to vomit—not unlike the feeling of nausea that was plaguing her at this very moment.

"Well there's no right or wrong way to start, but if you feel comfortable, you can sit." Dr. Cayden lifted her dainty hand and pointed a thin finger at the couch that sat adjacent to her chair.

This woman actually has a couch for the "crazy" people to sit on, Sierra thought.

Dr. Cayden was wearing a white, silk, long-sleeved shirt with a string of white pearls and a knee-length black pencil skirt. Black, narrow-toed heels adorned her neatly crossed feet, the right foot lying gently on top of the left.

Sierra definitely wasn't comfortable and didn't think that sitting would help with that, but she needed to do something with herself—she was feeling really anxious. The speed with which Dr. Cayden's secretary had gotten her in for this appointment had made her suspicious of this doctor's abilities. After all, if she was so amazing, shouldn't she be booked at least three months out? Ultimately, however, she'd realized that she would make any excuse not to come to this appointment that was making her so uncomfortable, so she'd decided to ignore her doubts.

Sierra sat down on the couch, amused by the fact that Dr. Cayden fit the description of the stereotypical psychologist, right down to the glasses and tightly wound bun of hair. The doctor sat with a half smile, waiting for Sierra to find her "comfort" spot.

Finally, Sierra stopped fidgeting.

"We could start by talking about why you're here," Dr. Cayden said.

Sierra took a deep breath and tried to relax. Although she wasn't particularly eager to "spill her guts" to a stranger, she also didn't want to waste the money she was paying this woman to listen to her spilling her guts. She looked around the room. The office itself was comforting. The walls were an oatmeal color that really didn't elicit any emotion at all. A picture of an orchid on the wall reminded Sierra of her own home, and that held comfort in and of itself. Dr. Cayden's undergraduate, graduate, and doctorate degrees also decorated the wall. Her desk sat behind her, oak and tidy. The air was fresh, and Sierra looked around for the air freshener that she was sure was plugged into the wall somewhere but found none. A window behind the doctor's desk overlooked the street below. It all looked very official.

Loosen up, Sierra. This is what you're here for.

"Well, I guess I'm here because I can't sleep," she finally responded. "No, that's not it," she amended. "The problem is I sleep too much."

Dr. Cayden's serene, very peaceful look seemed friendly enough, though she offered no smile. The doctor sat quietly and Sierra realized she was waiting for her to elaborate. So she rolled her shoulders back to try and relieve the tension there, took another deep breath, and continued.

"Well, it started about two months ago. I began to have these weird, very disturbing dreams. These dreams feel real. At first I couldn't get any sleep because I would dream some weird dream in the middle of the night and when I was able to wake myself up, I either didn't want to go back to sleep or I had so little time left to sleep that I would just get up and stay up. But then I would drag the rest of that day."

"Had you had trouble sleeping prior to these dreams occurring?"

"Actually, I've had trouble sleeping most of my adult life," Sierra admitted. "But it was never because of dreams. It was getting to sleep that was the problem."

"Why do you think that is?" Dr. Cayden asked, uncrossing her feet and then crossing them again so that now her left foot lay on top of the right.

Sierra shrugged. "I don't know. I guess I've always had a lot of things on my mind. I think about things I need to do and haven't done yet. I think about things I've done throughout the day and how I could have done them better. I think about all of this all day long, even when I'm working and doing the things I need to do. I guess I never really learned how to turn my mind off at bedtime." Sierra shrugged again after her revelation, as if in acceptance of what would always be.

Dr. Cayden nodded as though she understood something unspoken. "And now you sleep too much?"

"Yes, I do. I sleep—or rather, *have* slept in the recent past—for over fourteen hours. The sleep isn't restful, though."

Never changing her expression yet leaning forward, Dr. Cayden pressed Sierra. "You've slept over fourteen hours in a continuous period?"

"Uh, yes," Sierra said. "If the time could be broken up, I might have very little to complain about," she added with some sarcasm.

"And you felt tired after this long period of sleep."

"Yes, I did."

Dr. Cayden nodded. "Can you tell me about your dreams?"

Sierra was surprised the doctor seemed so unconcerned that she was sleeping for so many hours a day. The woman had a face of stone. *What kind of doctor is she?* she wondered—but she'd already decided to give the woman the benefit of the doubt, so she gathered her thoughts and started from the beginning.

"Well, one of the first dreams that I can recall, I was in a forest. It was dark and I was all by myself. I was surrounded by the sounds of nature and by trees. Above me was a starry sky. The stars were the only light I could see. I started to walk, but I had no idea which direction to go in. I tried to think of which star was the North Star, and maybe figure out a constellation to give me a hint." She pursed her lips. "For me, that was a surprising thought, because the only information I know about astronomy I learned in elementary school. I'm not sure I could guide myself anywhere based only on my knowledge of the stars. Yet the me in my dreams seemed to think that this was a viable option. I could think of nothing else. I felt scared and alone. I didn't even call out for help. It was so dark, and I didn't think any human would hear me—but I was pretty sure some hungry animal might. Instead, I just sat down near a tree and wept. I woke up then and cried for the rest of the night. That scared and lost feeling stayed with me even after I woke up." Sierra stopped her story there, lost in the memory.

"And what do you think that means?"

Sierra smiled to herself and looked past Dr. Cayden out

of the window. She stared at the building across the way. It was tall and made of brick the color of amber. She could see the windows in the building, but couldn't see into them. She couldn't tell what they did in that building across the street. Could they see her? Did they know that she was seeing this psychologist? Would they judge her now and think that she was crazy?

Dr. Cayden had just asked the quintessential question all the therapists on TV always asked. It had never made sense to Sierra before, just as it didn't make any sense now. If she knew what it meant, would she really need to be sitting in this office making herself uncomfortable? But all she said was, "I don't know what it means."

"What about the next couple of dreams you had following that first one?" Dr. Cayden asked, apparently nonplussed by Sierra's reply.

"In the next dream I can remember, I'm running. I'm not sure who I'm running from, but I know that I'm scared. I hear dogs barking and feet coming fast behind me."

Dr. Cayden nodded once, as if encouraging Sierra to continue.

Sierra related the rest of the events of the dream, finishing with, "And then a rope was around my neck and I was swinging from a tree. I had been lynched." She could feel tears coming to her eyes, and she wiped them away roughly with her hand until Dr. Cayden offered her a box of tissues. She took the box and sniffed. "Thank you."

"You're welcome," Dr. Cayden said. "Did you die in your dream?"

Sierra shook her head left and then right. "No, I don't

think so. I woke up just as I could feel the tightness of the cord around my neck and the warmth of the fire burning. I could hear laughter around me, though I couldn't see anything."

"How did this dream make you feel?"

Sierra thought for a moment. "It made me feel scared and alone. It made me feel powerless."

Dr. Cayden nodded again. "Do you have these dreams every night, where you feel powerless?"

"No, not every night. Especially in the beginning—they would only happen about two or three times a week, and they would never last very long. I would always wake up just when things were getting really bad. In most of the dreams I was some character from the past." Sierra blew her nose. "The dream I had after the lynching dream was in a cotton field. I was a slave and I was surrounded by others. Actually, it was the first dream where I wasn't alone. I mean, I didn't know the people in the dream, but somehow I knew that we were all connected. I am always myself in the dreams, like I am now. Or, rather, my thoughts are my own, but the people around me are seeing me as someone else. I'm always dressed according to where I am and what I'm doing. All the people around me are from that time period, and they call me by a different name, but I still have my own thoughts, how they are today."

"What happened at the end of the dream in the cotton field?"

"I was beaten with a whip because I was accused of not doing my share of the work."

"And were you sad and scared again, like you were before?"

"No, actually, I was pissed off. I mean maybe I was a little scared, but mostly I was angry. Maybe I was angry enough to forget that I should be scared. But I wasn't able to do anything with that anger. It all happened quickly, and then I was awake again."

"And who were you angry at?"

Sierra almost got angry then, as the doctor posed what Sierra felt was another dumb question. She kept her temper in check. "I was angry at the man holding the whip and bringing down lashes on my back."

Dr. Cayden nodded again. "I see."

Sierra was getting frustrated and angry. "What do you see? If you see a reason and a solution, then by all means, please share."

Dr. Cayden didn't respond immediately. Sierra couldn't understand why she felt so upset, but she was becoming increasingly irritated by the doctor's questions.

"Do you ever feel out of place in your everyday life?" Dr. Cayden asked. She was talking as if she hadn't sensed Sierra's change of mood.

"I don't know," Sierra said. "I guess, sometimes. But I don't understand the relevance. I mean, I think most people feel out of place sometimes in their everyday lives."

"And is it only sometimes that you feel out of place in your own life?"

Sierra took her time and really thought about the question. She could see where the doctor was going, finally, with this line of questioning. She really thought she knew herself, at least up until the last couple of months. Lately, though, it seemed like she'd been questioning everything about her existence, including her happiness in the life that she'd created for herself. *Do I really fit into my own life?* She wasn't sure anymore.

"I don't know," she said. "I just don't know. I mean, I thought I knew, but lately I don't know."

"All right. Well that's a question that I want you to consider. This was a very good start today. When was the last time that you had one of these dreams?" Dr. Cayden uncrossed her ankles as if preparing to get up.

Sierra looked down at her cell phone and realized that they had already spent fifty minutes together. "The last dream was actually this weekend. I really haven't had any problems this week." Sierra smiled at her reply, reminding herself that the week had just begun.

"Sierra, I want to know what your expectations are in coming to therapy," Dr. Cayden said. "What do you hope you'll get out of this?"

Sierra was at first thrown off by the question, and took a moment to answer. Finally, she said, "I guess I'm just hoping for some understanding as to why I'm having these dreams, and hoping I can get help to make them stop."

"Very good," Dr. Cayden said. "I just want to make sure your goals are realistic and something we can aspire to."

Sierra did the nodding in understanding this time.

"I want you to come see me at least once a week to start off," Dr. Cayden went on. "I'm certainly concerned with your excessive sleeping, and these types of things are usually due to some stress or unresolved issue in your life. Your dreams may be telling you something about yourself that you're addressing in your subconscious but not ready to face in your reality."

"Well, okay then," Sierra said as she got up from the couch, eager to leave.

"I also think that it would be a good idea for you to start keeping a journal or diary. You don't have to feel pressured to write in it every day, but it may help you to decipher your feelings."

Sierra tensed a little at this, but nodded in agreement.

"I'm also going to encourage you to get into a space of relaxation before you go to sleep. I want you to light candles, maybe take a bath—whatever relaxes you—and see if that helps with your sleeping. Turn off the television an hour before you go to sleep and try to get into a quiet space."

"Sure, okay," Sierra said.

This experience hadn't been as painful as she'd thought it might be. The session had actually made her feel kind of free, talking about what was going on with her. She thought once a week seemed a little excessive, but she was willing to give this therapy thing a shot.

Dr. Cayden met her as she got to her feet and shook her hand. Only then did the doctor let out a genuine, full smile. Her handshake was firm, which Sierra appreciated.

"I have an emergency line if you need to contact me after hours," Dr. Cayden said. "You can leave a message, and I'll be sure to get back to you."

"Thank you," Sierra said.

And with that, the session was over. Sierra walked out of the room and into the small reception area outside.

"Miss Donovan, did you want to go ahead and schedule your next appointment?" asked the receptionist, a very friendly blonde with twinkling blue eyes and smooth, pale, porcelain skin. She exuded the type of happiness and cheer that made Sierra wonder if this young woman had ever had a real problem in her life. According to the name tag on her desk, her name was Gail.

"Sure," Sierra replied, and she took out her phone to check her schedule for a free day the following week. "Friday afternoon?"

"Perfect," Gail said. She continued to smile as she entered the appointment in the computer. "Have a good day!" she called out as Sierra walked away.

As Sierra made her way to her car, she decided she would take the doctor's words to heart. She needed to try and figure out if she really was happy with her life—and if she wasn't, she needed to see if she could do something to make things different.

Chapter 11

Sierra sat in her car mentally reviewing and logging her time with Dr. Cayden. She realized that she'd revealed more to that woman in one hour than she had ever told anyone. Having let loose made her feel very uneasy, even if she also had a sense of freedom after talking about the dreams and her life.

Suddenly, she wasn't sure she really wanted to think about her life and whether or not she was happy. Thinking about her present life would ultimately lead to thoughts about her past, and she didn't want that. She never wanted that. Yet the thoughts were overwhelming her now. She was remembering the smells, the sounds—and then she remembered the attic.

It was late in the afternoon. The sun was slowly going down, but she didn't even notice. She was with her friend Diana, and everything was right with the world. Playing in the attic was so mysterious. She ran among the empty boxes, the material from some old lace dress grazing her arm as she ran by. Her friend was far ahead. She was trying to catch her. Diana was a beautiful little girl. She had light brown skin and black hair.

Diana always shared her toys and books, even her favorite candies, with Sierra, and Sierra adored her. They always played in the attic together; it was the only place in the house where they were allowed to run. Two uninhibited six-year-old girls enjoying the freedom of play. Now, Sierra was trying to catch up with her friend, and she finally did. They had come to an open door, and behind it was Diana's older cousin, Wayne, who lived with them.

"Hey," he said. "What are you guys doing?"

"We're just playing," Diana said.

"Diana, go play over there for a while," Wayne said. He pointed to the far corner of the attic.

"Okay," Diana said, and she began to make her way to the other side of the attic with Sierra trailing behind.

But Wayne grabbed Sierra's hand. "Why don't you come with me?"

"No, I want to go with Diana," Sierra said.

"I have some candy for you," Wayne said. He gave her a big smile. "Just come play with me for a second."

"No, thank you," Sierra responded, hoping that her politeness would be enough to deter him. She knew what his kind of play meant, and she wanted no part of it. She began to back away to the corner of the attic, where her friend was engaging in the only kind of "play" she wanted any part of.

Wayne grabbed her arm when she didn't budge and began to pull her toward him.

"Come here, I just need to show you something really quick."

Just when Sierra was about to raise the volume of her voice to try and alert her friend, Wayne bent down and whispered harshly in her ear, "Do you remember what I told you? If you tell anybody, I will kill your family. Do you want that? Do you want your family dead?"

Terror reached down into Sierra's chest and made it hard to breathe, let alone form words. All she could do was shake her head no.

"Good," Wayne said. "Then come and see what I have for you. And then you can go play."

Okay," Sierra relented in a teary voice.

Wayne opened a small door Sierra had never noticed before and waved his hand as an invitation for her to enter. When she did, he immediately gave her the candy he'd promised.

Sierra took the candy and began to unwrap it, hoping that this was all he had for her but knowing in her heart that it wasn't.

In the middle of the room was a table with a blanket covering it up. Wayne helped Sierra onto it. He said for this game she would have to lie down, and so, tentatively, thinking she had no other option, she did, the candy gripped firmly in her hand. In the next moment, Wayne was pulling her pants down, and Sierra realized his were already down.

"What are you doing?" she asked, recoiling. "I don't like this game."

"Relax," he said. "It's almost over." He held her hands to her sides, and she felt something hard pushing against her private place.

Wayne kept pushing for what felt like forever to Sierra, but what may have only been a couple of seconds. She could hear Wayne mumbling under his breath, "This isn't working." Sierra was uncomfortable, scared, and ashamed. This wasn't right, she knew it. She could hear Diana calling her name faintly in the background. Wayne must have heard it too, because he gave up on the pushing and began to touch himself. Sierra was very confused.

By this time, she could hear Diana on the other side of the door, loud and clear, begging for entry and the return of her playmate.

Wayne told Sierra that she was a good girl and wiped between her legs before pulling her pants up and returning her to Diana. Afterward, Sierra continued to play, even with the pain between her legs. She was confused, but glad to be back with her friend and away from Wayne.

⌒

Sitting there in her car, Sierra began to rock back and forth. It had been a long time since she had even thought about that experience, and she wasn't relishing the reflection. She chastised herself for selling her soul for a piece of candy. She put her head between her arms, held on to the steering wheel for support, and counted in her head while she took deep breaths and willed her breathing to steady. She knew this feeling. She felt like she was going to die. It was another panic attack.

"You're okay," she said out loud. "You're okay." She made it a chant, a plea, that she repeated again and again.

After several minutes she felt normal again—the only normal she knew. The feeling passed, just as it always did. She finally turned the key in the ignition and pulled off.

Chapter 12

Dear Diary (I guess that's what people write),

It's been an ordinary day so far. Last night I slept and still haven't had one of my dreams again. And I've been able to avoid thoughts from the past. The visit to Dr. Cayden really shook me up, and I'm not sure I'm looking forward to my appointment on Friday.

I don't know. I think that I might have been working too hard and that might be the reason for my dreams and near nervous breakdown. I'm just too young to feel this old. Anyway, this week thus far has been successful at work. I found a house just off the lake for the older couple so I have that commission, and then of course I worked with other clients, including Steve. Steve. He's pretty good looking—not that it matters, diary, but let's face it, the man is fine. He is, in fact, the most handsome man I know. I mean ...

Right in the middle of her last thought, Sierra heard the phone ring.

She had just bought a journal to log her thoughts throughout the day, as Dr. Cayden had suggested. She was hoping it would help her unscramble her mind, which was totally confused these days. It had been years since she'd even considered taking a vacation, but she would definitely take one now—just as soon as she found Steve a house, or after he decided to make an offer on the one that he'd seemed so interested in the last time they were together.

Sierra checked the caller ID on her cell phone. *Mom.* She answered.

"Hey, Mom."

"Hey, baby. How you been?"

"I'm good, Mama. What's up with you?"

"Oh, nothing, baby. I'm just blessed and grateful to be alive. But I called to make sure you were all right. You haven't been returning my calls like you should, and I gave you some space only because your sister told me about the dreams you've been having and that you wanted to be left alone."

Sierra took in what her mom was saying and shook her head at the fact that her mom and sister were talking about her behind her back. The fact was, she *always* wanted to be left alone, but these two wouldn't stop meddling if she paid them.

"Mama, I'm fine. It's nothing that I can't handle, and I'm handling it okay." *Please, let that be enough*, Sierra pleaded silently.

Pearl sighed in resignation. "I'll let it go," she said. "As long as you promise to learn how to return a phone call within a twenty-four-hour period."

"Fine, Mama," Sierra agreed, now smiling.

"Anyways, that's not why I called. I called to ask if you've been out with Dale yet."

It took a second for Sierra to even recall who Dale was. *Oh yes, that's right—the setup.* Only now did she remember that she was supposed to call him back and hadn't. She really didn't want to pass this information on to her mother, however. She knew that would just open up the floodgates of investigation.

"Well, uhh, not yet. We had a date planned but had to break it."

"You haven't talked to him since then? You guys haven't rescheduled?"

"No, Mama, we haven't," Sierra reluctantly admitted.

"Well, don't wait too long. He seems like a very nice young man, and you really don't get out enough. You need to try and give somebody a chance. It's not right being by yourself so much and at your age. You should be getting those feelers out to see if you can find a husband. That might be why you're having the bad dreams."

Oh my goodness! Sierra screamed in her head. She so wanted to hang up the phone and end this conversation, but that was not an option. She respected her mother too much to ever hang up on her. And somewhere deep inside, she also knew that this conversation was coming from a concerned-parent kind of place.

"I want you to promise that you'll call him today and reschedule your date."

"Oh, come on, Mama. I'll call him when I get a chance." Sierra wanted to point out to her mom that Dale was obviously not pressed about the date himself because he hadn't called to reschedule, either—but then a vague memory of seeing a follow-up text from him about a week after their broken date came to her. *Whoops.*

"No," Pearl said. "I already know what that means when you say it, and I want you to promise me that you'll call him today. Like when you get off the phone with me."

Pearl faced complete silence on the other end of the phone, as Sierra didn't know what to say.

"Come on, do this for your mom who loves you so much and just wants to see you happy."

Sierra hated when her mom used that line about loving her so much during negotiations. Coming from her, those words held a lot of power.

"Fine, I promise. Okay," Sierra blurted out in frustration.

"Good. Now, baby, did you eat today?"

Sierra's mom carried on with her regular line of questioning about what Sierra had been eating and how work was going for another half hour. Then, finally, she said she had to go because she had errands to run—but not before reminding Sierra of her promise to call Dale.

When she hung up with her mom, Sierra put the phone back down on the table and looked at her hands, as if they would hold the answer to whether or not she should call Dale right now or later.

Studying the lines on her hands, she traced the lines on her palms as they started on one side of her hand and then disappeared between her fingers. She'd heard people call these lines "life lines" before. The longer these lines were, the longer you were supposed to live, or something like that. She couldn't really remember right now. What she was beginning to realize was that life was short and if she wasn't careful, it would pass her by.

"Okay, I'll call now," she decided aloud.

She picked her cell phone back up and found Dale in her contact list, then quickly pressed the enter button to dial his number before she decided not to do it.

The phone rang, and after about two rings, a male voice said, "Hello?"

"Hello. Is this Dale?" Sierra asked tentatively.

"Yes, it is."

"Hey, Dale. This is Sierra, giving you a call back."

"Sierra, Sierra . . ." Dale repeated, as if trying to remind himself who she was. And then he said with a laugh, "Just kidding! Hey, Sierra, I didn't think that you would call me back. I thought maybe you were mad because I had to cancel."

Sierra found that hilarious, remembering how relieved she'd been that he had canceled. But instead of revealing that information, she simply said, "No, I wasn't angry. Actually, I was calling to see if you wanted to reschedule."

"Sure, definitely," Dale agreed without hesitation. "What are you doing tomorrow night?"

Sierra thought about it and realized the next day would be Friday. She had nothing to do on Friday night. The thought ran across her mind that maybe she should pretend she had to check a schedule, so that Dale wouldn't think she had no life. But she wanted to turn over a new leaf. She would be up front and clear. "Sure, tomorrow night would be fine. Let's say around eight."

"Sounds good," Dale replied.

"Okay, well, I'll talk to you later then."

"Okay," Dale said, amusement evident in his voice.

"Okay, bye," Sierra quickly said, and she disconnected the call.

For some reason she had thought there was no way Dale would want to make another date; she hadn't been prepared for him to say yes to rescheduling. But she had to go through with it now. She would just have to try and control her anxiety about all the other things going on in her life and go out on a date with this guy.

Well, at least she had something to do this Friday night. It would either be enjoyable or a disaster—but either way, the outing would be a distraction from all of the very serious thoughts battling inside of her head.

Chapter 13

*D*ay turned into night and light became darkness. As Dr. Cayden had instructed, Sierra began to attempt to get in a relaxed space before going to sleep. She turned the lights down in her bedroom and bathroom and placed scented lavender candles all around both the spaces. After a nice, long bubble bath, she changed into her most comfortable cotton nightgown and lay down in her bed. She felt her eyes start to droop, and she pulled the covers and comforter tight around her. Her whole body settled down.

When she opened her eyes again, she saw an easel in front of her. That was the very first thing that Sierra noticed. The second was that she was no longer in the sweet comfort of her home. She looked around and saw that she was at a river's edge, surrounded by trees bursting with foliage. The air around her was alive. She could hear the sounds of the forest. The birds were singing as they flew through the trees celebrating their freedom. The insects bustled around, shaking the leaves and moving through the dirt, accomplishing their day's work. The water streamed through the rocks, alive and creating life. The river's song settled her even as she struggled to gather her thoughts.

Sierra was sitting on a quilt of greens, blues, and grays that acted as camouflage against the floor of the forest. She was wearing the same dress she had been wearing at the church in her last dream. In front of her was a canvas that featured the woods around her. The painting captured the essence of the forest while still allowing the observer to see the peace and tranquility the artist felt from interacting with this backdrop.

Sierra stared at the painting for a moment, so absorbed in appreciating it that she almost forgot that she hadn't yet determined where she was or why she was here. She had only gotten so far as to deduce that she must be dreaming again.

She admired the painting for a few moments. She appreciated the artist's brushstrokes, and his or her ability to see what others might not so readily see. She looked around to discover who might be the owner of the painting, and realized that she was holding a paintbrush.

Recognition came in that second. *She* was the painter. This canvas belonged to her.

Noticing the oil paints lying on the quilt, she slowly dipped her brush into the dark green. The shade was already perfectly blended to translate the green in the foliage of the tree that stood in front of her. She allowed her hand to move. For the moment, she didn't care if this was a dream. She enjoyed the jolt of exhilaration that came as her brush touched the canvas, and she began to make slow strokes. She felt her spirit soar and her mind emancipate itself.

She was so caught up in painting that she didn't notice the rustle going through the trees until it grew loud enough to demand her attention, even in her lost state. Suddenly apprehensive, Sierra went perfectly still. It instantly occurred to her that in her dreams, she always had to be ready for anything. Even when she experienced calm, chaos was never far behind. She put the paintbrush down and braced herself for what would happen next.

"Dorothy, Dorothy, where are you?" a concerned male voice called out.

Sierra continued to be silent, not yet ready to reveal her location to whomever was asking. But even without her response, the voice got closer and closer and continued to call for her.

Sierra sighed and marveled at the persistence of this stranger. She stood up and moved away from the blanket, closer to the riverbed. She still refused to call out.

After a few minutes, she saw the greenery being brushed back, and a male figure burst forth.

Even as she registered that she had met this man before, he rushed toward her and grabbed her in a hug that lifted her off her feet and spun her around. Sierra had no real option but to hold on tight. Before putting her down, the man dipped her over his arm and kissed her lips with a sincerity that convinced Sierra she would have probably swooned had he not been holding her. When he released his hold a little, it was only to make enough room to look into her eyes.

Sierra gazed back and was surprised by how familiar those eyes were. She knew this man. He was the handsome charmer from the house in the last dream. But even with that knowledge, she recognized that her heart, although beating irregularly, also acknowledged him. This man was something more than a stranger.

Knowledge such as this would normally strike fear into Sierra's heart. This time, however, she wasn't afraid—she was intrigued. She didn't yet know if her courage was coming from her recognition that this was, in fact, a dream, or if the man himself set her mind at rest.

As Sierra pondered these questions, the man took his finger and ran it across the lips he had just kissed.

"Dorothy, didn't you hear me calling you?"

Sierra understood that she was meant to answer, but she didn't really know what to say, so she merely nodded and continued to stare. She watched as worry entered his eyes.

He put a finger under her chin and tilted her face up toward his. "Are you feeling okay?"

Again, Sierra only nodded, but this time she added a shaky smile, hoping to put him at ease. She had known from the moment she saw him that he would never physically hurt her—and now, staring into his eyes, she was awestruck at the affection that was evident in them. Sierra thought the emotion might be love, but she hadn't had enough experience with that feeling to be sure.

She finally found her voice and responded. "I'm okay."

This seemed to bring relief to her admirer, and he was able to finally release her. As he did, he reached into a satchel that Sierra hadn't even realized he was holding.

Freed from the power of his gaze, she took the opportunity to fully take him in. He was tall, with dark skin and thick black hair that was cut neatly into an Afro. He had on a crisp, white, short-sleeved dress shirt and black dress pants that were neatly pressed.

"I came to get you. It's almost time for the meeting. I've

been going over a few ideas, things that we could try and do differently on our next march. I also have some thoughts about how we could get more people to try and register to vote."

The man continued to talk as if he and Sierra were picking up a conversation that they had put down. She struggled to catch up.

"The march and voting?" Sierra asked, openly trying to understand.

He gave Sierra an odd look before answering. "Yes, Dorothy. We're supposed to go out tomorrow and try again to get people to vote. These white folks got people so scared that I don't know how many people are going to even open their doors and hear us out. But we've got to keep trying, right?"

"Right," Sierra said, answering him mostly to keep the conversation going.

She remembered talking with her grandmother about when workers came to her town in Mississippi and labored to get black people to register to vote. Even as the man continued to talk, she allowed her eyes to drift to the river. It looked similar to the one that ran by her grandmother's house. The memory of speaking to her grandmother about— well, about *anything* brought a smile to Sierra's face, as her grandmother had long ago passed away. But a slight frown quickly followed when she remembered the danger that was attached to trying to vote during that time.

"Dorothy, where are you? You've got this funny, faraway look. Are you even listening?"

Sierra shook her head to try and gain some focus, and then she struggled to answer him. "I'm listening, um . . . umm." She had no idea what his name was.

"Are you sure you're feeling all right? If I didn't know any better, I would think that you'd forgotten my name." He lovingly touched her cheek, and smiled playfully as he said, "I'm John, your man, remember?"

"I remember," Sierra said immediately. And even as she said it, she knew it was true.

John seemed satisfied with her reply; he let her go and walked over to her painting. "I see you've created another masterpiece," he said, his voice full of admiration.

Sierra beamed with pleasure from the compliment and walked over to the canvas as they looked on together.

"Your talent really amazes me. You are really something special, you know that?"

Again, Sierra didn't know what to do with the praise, so she just put it away inside herself.

John turned and held her in his arms again in a way that was becoming more and more familiar to Sierra. He released her slowly again and then that smile rose up once more, as if he was sharing a secret with her—only she didn't know what it was yet. Then he reached in his pocket, pulled something out, and cupped it in his hand.

"I have something for you," he said.

"What is it?" Sierra asked.

"It's a surprise. I want you to close your eyes for me."

Sierra hesitated for only a second before obediently closing her eyes, putting her trust in her dream man.

Once her eyes were closed, she felt his hands lightly graze her neck and then felt the sensation of something small and a little cold hanging against her breastbone.

"Okay, now open your eyes," John whispered.

Sierra looked down and saw her gift: a gold charm in the shape of a heart, suspended by a gold chain that hung just below her sternum. She looked up at John and his eyes were filled with kindness and a little worry. When she remained silent, his eyebrows began to furrow.

"Do you like it?" he finally asked.

Sierra then grasped that she had yet to speak. She was touched by the charm more than she could say. She wasn't sure she had the words to fully express her feelings so she went with her initial thought. "It's beautiful."

John seemed to let out the breath that he was holding, and the signs of concern on his face melted away like snow in the spring. "Good!" he said. "Now, you and the world can know that you carry my heart with you everywhere you go." And then he smiled with his whole person, and Sierra knew that she had never seen anyone light up in that way.

John held her again and gave her a sweet kiss, and his warmth seeped into her and lit a small flame that started in her toes and gradually went to her head, making her cheeks flush.

As they moved away from each other, they stared at one another and frantically tried to catch their breath. After a few minutes, they were able to breathe normally again. Sierra was a little amused at their labored panting, and John seemed to be as well.

John was the first to speak. "Come on, we need to get ready for service."

Sierra's confusion translated in her response. "What service?"

John shook his head. "I see I can't leave you alone too

long. You start to paint and just forget everything." He took the sting out of his words with the honey in his voice.

Sierra smiled.

"We have service tonight at the church and then afterward we're going to meet and talk about our plans for tomorrow with the voter registration drive," John explained, all patience.

Sierra watched him as he walked over to her quilt and very carefully began to pick up and pack away her paint supplies. She went over to help. The paintbrush that she was holding before John came grabbed her attention and she picked it up, and as she did, the sound of the river's flowing seemed to turn up its volume. Its melody hypnotized Sierra and she walked toward the water's edge with the brush in hand. She bent down and immersed the paintbrush in the water, watching the green fade into the dark waters. And then there were just dark waters. And then there was nothing.

Chapter 14

$\mathcal{F}$riday brought along sunshine and warmer temperatures for an early spring morning in Milwaukee. Sierra, happily surprised, welcomed the warm glow invading her bedroom through the window. She had to admit that the previous night's dream hadn't been a nightmare at all. The dream had left her feeling excited and a little rejuvenated. She didn't know whether the painting or the man in the dream was what made her feel so energized. She imagined that the cause was probably a little bit of both. She could still remember John's eyes, though for some reason she couldn't remember anything else about his face. She was sure that she had looked into those gentle eyes before—in another life, maybe.

She enjoyed a long, languid stretch and let out a nice high-pitched sound to go along with it. She was smiling as she got ready to face her day. The smile stayed on her face as she placed her feet on the floor.

The night before, she had really worked herself up thinking about her date with Dale. She had been anxious, and had spent the evening going back and forth between whether she would go or simply cancel. She felt uncomfortable about it yesterday, but with the warm feeling of her dream to buoy her, she was feeling much better today. She told herself that she would give herself the afternoon to think about what would be best; for now, she had a meeting with Steve.

Steve wanted to go and see the same house again. When they'd spoken on the phone the previous day, he'd asked her to meet him outside of the property around twelve thirty, which Sierra assumed was his lunch break.

Until then, Sierra had the morning to herself. She decided as she was washing her face that she would go to an art supply store and get some oils, brushes, and a canvas to work on. *Why not?* she thought. *I'll start a little vacation right here in the city.*

She had a long, hot shower and took her time getting dressed afterward in dark jeans, a canary-yellow cashmere sweater, and her high, black, soft-leather boots.

Sierra looked at her cell phone on the way out the door and couldn't believe that it was nine in the morning. She couldn't remember the last time she'd left the house so late.

The art supply store didn't open until ten, so she decided to take a drive around the lakefront. She always found it quite pleasant and moving to look at the vastness of Lake Michigan. It brought her instant peace.

She drove the winding road that curved around the lake, once, and then twice, before finally deciding to get herself to the art store. Once there, she picked out a cornucopia of colors, along with an array of brushes, an easel, and a canvas. She decided that she would paint with oil, a medium she had always enjoyed. She felt good as she got in the car and headed over to Brown Deer to meet Steve at the house.

❦

Sierra reached the house about an hour early, so she pulled out her journal to do a little writing while she waited in the car for Steve.

Dear Diary,

Well, I haven't had any nightmares in a couple of weeks, although I have had dreams. In the dreams I feel as though I've been learning something about myself and the kind of person I want to be. Maybe the nightmares have gone away because I've learned all that they could teach me. They showed me that I have been unhappy, taking the blessings in my life for granted and really not living up to my full potential as a person.

But I don't think I've figured out what my full potential is, or even what it is that would make me happy. I mean—don't get me wrong—on the one hand, the dreams were scary and disturbing. But, on the other hand, the person in the dreams lately is a fearless woman, a woman of action and strength. She is a helper and giver and is confident in who she is and what she should do. That's definitely not me yet. Maybe one day, but not yet.

A knock on her driver's window made Sierra jump in her seat. It was Steve, staring at her with a smile on his face. She smiled back before she even knew she was doing it and brought her hand down from her chest, where she had placed it after her scare. She grabbed the door handle and pulled the lever as Steve moved out of the way.

"I'm sorry. I didn't mean to scare you," he immediately told her as she stepped out of the car.

Instantly, Sierra felt a little déjà vu, as the words mirrored what had happened at their last meeting. "It's fine, no problem. So, shall we?" she asked. Without waiting for an answer, she closed the car door, hit the lock button on her key fob, and headed toward the property. She moved so fast that Steve had to rush to keep up with her.

The front lawn was still inviting with its well-kept grass and red-bricked walkway leading straight to the front door.

Keys in her hand, Sierra turned to Steve before opening the door. "So, do you think you've come to a decision about the place?"

"Actually, I think I have. I just want to take one last look before I make a final decision."

"Great," Sierra exclaimed a little too cheerily as she opened the door and then walked in all the way to allow Steve access to enter the house behind her. She was feeling very nervous around him. As soon as she'd seen him outside her car window, her stomach had started doing flips and her heart had begun to beat fast. She had been thinking about him since the last time they were together, although she didn't want to admit it. And now seeing him again was doing funny things to her insides. She needed some fresh air and some space.

Already heading for the kitchen, she called behind her, "I'll give you a chance to look around again and familiarize yourself with the house. If you have any questions, just let me know."

"I actually wanted to get your opinion on a couple of things if you don't mind," Steve said quickly.

Sierra stopped in her tracks, then pivoted and retraced her steps back to Steve's side. "Umm. Sure. That's no problem. What do you need my opinion on?"

"Uh . . ." Steve walked toward the living room, and

beckoned with his hand for Sierra to follow. "I was wondering what kind of table would fit in here, and do you think I could possibly set up an entertainment center along this wall?" He pointed to the wall adjacent to the entrance, which looked as if it was made for a television and entertainment center.

Sierra was a little confused at his apparent cluelessness but happy to say something that might get him to make up his mind. "Yes," she said, "this area is definitely made for an entertainment center." She gestured to the space next to her. "I think you could get a coffee table in here as well, along with a couch, loveseat, and any other furniture you might want to set up. It's very spacious and open to all different kinds of interpretations."

Sierra finished her spiel and then smiled at Steve encouragingly—only the way Steve was looking at her was sending shivers down her spine. A part of her still wanted to deny it, but she wasn't a complete idiot. This man was attracted to her, and he didn't seem to feel the need to hide it today. An electricity was in the air that couldn't be denied. She really, really wanted to get away from him. This attraction was inappropriate, and she hadn't closed the deal yet. She needed to break eye contact, like now.

Dragging her eyes away from his gaze, she tried to ease the tension that had all of a sudden filled the room. "Was there anything else that you needed my opinion on?" she asked, looking anywhere but at him.

"Actually, yes, there is. If you could just follow me." Steve walked out of the living room back into the foyer space and began to climb the hardwood stairs to the second floor.

Sierra reluctantly followed, holding on to the smoothness

of the oakwood banister to try and maintain composure. It seemed that the longer she was around him, the more she was attracted to him. She was feeling really flustered at this point, but she was a professional and was determined to shake off this crazy feeling. Still, she couldn't help glancing at his back as they climbed the stairs—his strong, broad back, which matched perfectly with his broad shoulders and muscular arms. This man definitely worked out, and his skin was the most beautiful ebony—and it was so smooth. His hair was cut so it was nicely tapered, jet black, perfect . . . *And I should get my mind straight and stop staring at this man.*

They reached the top of the stairs and the hallway opened into three different directions. The white walls welcomed entrance to the left and to the right. Steve went to the right, away from the master bedroom, for which Sierra was very, very grateful. He opened up the door to the smallest of the four bedrooms and walked in and around the room.

The walls in here were red, and the room housed a large picture window that looked out into the backyard. The windowsill was big enough for cushions for seating, and Sierra suddenly imagined herself looking out the window at the pale moonlight and painting the brilliance of the sky. She walked over and sat down on the windowsill so that she was facing the open room and Steve. "So, what was your question?"

Steve shook his head a bit, a bemused look on his face. "I'm sorry, what?"

Sierra smiled and repeated her question. "You said you had some questions about this room. What were they?"

Steve seemed to scour his brain for a moment, and then he said, "What would you do with this room?"

"What would *I* do with this room?"

He nodded.

She pondered the question. "Well . . ." Sierra smiled to herself, thinking about the oil paints that she had in the car. "I would make it a study or hobby room."

"Do you have a specific hobby in mind?"

"Actually, I do. I would make this room my painting room, almost like my very own studio. I love this picture window and I love the color of the room."

Sierra couldn't believe that she'd shared that; she told almost nobody about her passion for painting. She'd put that side of her away inside of herself a long time ago so she could concentrate on her advertising and real estate. She was quite surprised that she would share this part of herself with a person who was almost a stranger. But there was something in Steve's eyes that seemed so warm and open.

"So you paint." Steve jumped right on that bit of information.

"I haven't in a long time but I'm starting again," Sierra said.

"Why haven't you painted in a long time? I mean, you clearly enjoy it. Your face lit up as soon as the words left your mouth."

Sierra was disconcerted about the fact that the conversation was all of a sudden about her. *Change the subject.* "I don't know. I guess I just haven't had the time. But this isn't about me, this is about you. So what do *you* think of the room?"

Steve slowly nodded his head and looked around the room once again. "I really like this room. I think it definitely opens up a person's sense of creativity." He looked in her direction. "And I really like the view."

Ignoring the leading comment, Sierra decided to turn it around. "Yes, the view from the window is very nice."

Steve laughed at this statement, though Sierra wasn't sure why. She decided not to pursue the matter. They had gotten personal enough for one day. She led the way out of the room and back into the upstairs hallway. "So, have you seen enough?"

"Yes, I've seen enough and I'll take it," Steve said.

Sierra noticed the reluctance in his voice, and wondered briefly what its source was—but her excitement over closing the deal trumped her curiosity. Manically jumping up and down for joy in her mind, she calmly put her hand out to Steve. "Congratulations!"

Steve took her hand in his and let her small fingers curl around his bigger ones.

Once again, Sierra felt that jolt go through her body at their contact, and she tried to release his hand as quickly and efficiently as possible. This time, Steve was willing to let it go, and Sierra took the opportunity to lead the way back down the stairs.

"Well, I'll go ahead and draw up the necessary papers and get the closing started," she said as they reached the bottom of the stairs. "I want to congratulate you again on your purchase."

"Well, thank you so much for all of your help."

"You're welcome. After all, it is my job," Sierra joked and laughed.

Steve responded with a huge smile.

She quickly made her way back to the front door, praying that Steve would follow her lead. She didn't like the intimacy she was feeling being around him. The problem wasn't that she was scared of him; she was more afraid of how he made her feel. She had never felt a connection like this before in her life, and she didn't know how to handle it. Steve was also still her client, and the way he was affecting her was completely unacceptable in her book.

It seemed that Steve could take a hint; he followed Sierra out the door without a word. But as they exited the property along the brick walkway, he touched her arm to stop her progression and said, "Hey, how about we go celebrate? I mean, I'm feeling really good, and it would be a treat for me to be able to buy you lunch as a thank-you."

Sierra's first instinct was to say no. "There's really no need to thank me. It's my job to find houses for my clients. Anyway, you realize that I get a commission from this sale, right? That's all the thanks I need," Sierra said. She flashed a weak smile. "And besides, don't you have to get back to school?"

"Actually, I took the rest of the day off."

Sierra frowned. "Why would you do that?"

"Because I didn't know how long I'd need to look at the house and make my final decision today. So, how about it?" Steve lifted his eyebrows. He looked hopeful.

Sierra sighed as she felt herself wanting to give in. As much as this man messed with her equilibrium, she thought he was a nice person and was really happy that they'd found him a place that worked for him. On the other hand, he was a client, and she didn't want him to get the wrong idea.

"Look, you're my client and I would really like to keep this professional—"

"Hey, I'm just saying, let's have lunch and maybe talk about the sale and celebrate a little. I promise my invitation is completely innocent."

Chapter 15

Sierra chose a little sandwich shop right around the corner from where they were, wanting to avoid the situation appearing too much like a date. They each got turkey clubs and soup.

Steve opened doors, pulled out chairs, and was as attentive as any woman could ask for. Sierra was impressed. He had an air about him that put her at ease, and he was extremely easy to talk to. She hadn't expected that, and she was completely disarmed—so much so that she started talking about her time at the ad agency and her current work. She talked about her parents, her siblings, and even her painting. She was so comfortable that she almost started talking about her dreams, but she caught herself just in time.

She had never meant to begin a friendship with Steve, and now she felt self-conscious about the amount of information she was sharing without knowing why. She felt a little raw and exposed—but she also felt a sense of freedom. She was generally a very private person; she rarely shared things about herself with her own family, let alone with strangers. Making friends was hard for her. She saw vulnerability as a weakness. Yet something else was going on here, and she didn't understand what it was.

The conversation was by no means one-sided. Sierra learned that Steve taught fifth grade and had always wanted to be a teacher. Both of his parents were in education. His mom was a principal in the Milwaukee public school system, and his father was a former superintendent in the same system who had written a book about education and now worked as a consultant for school boards and schools around the country.

Steve shared that he had never been married but had once been engaged. The engagement was broken off when they both realized that they ultimately wanted different things out of life. He had no children but wanted them. Essentially, he was currently living his dream and now just wanted to lay down some roots.

"So, how is it that you're able to get away from work in the middle of the day so often?" Sierra asked.

"I actually almost never take off work, certainly not any time in the last two years, so a couple of days now didn't really raise any eyebrows. Plus, I have a teaching assistant who helps out when needed."

"Yeah, but wouldn't it have just been easier to tell me to wait until the weekend?"

Steve sat back in his chair and gave Sierra a long look, as if he was trying to read her thoughts. "After the first time you disappeared and weren't returning phone calls, I realized I missed you and was harboring feelings other than client to real estate agent," he admitted. "I wanted to see you. I didn't want to wait."

Sierra's mouth dropped open at the admission. "You

wanted to see me enough to take off work . . . something you rarely do? But you don't even know me!"

Unrepentant, Steve simply returned her gaze steadily—then he smiled and said, "Plus, I really need a new house. My lease will be up in the next month."

His joking manner broke the tension, and Sierra was able to relax again.

She found herself marveling at how well the lunch was going. Steve was really funny. She was having such a good time, in fact, that she didn't realize how late it was until she checked her phone. They had been talking for two hours, and she had paperwork to complete and one more house to show that afternoon. She stood up and began to gather the remains of their lunch to place in the trash.

"I'm so sorry to rush off, but I really have to go," she said.

Steve looked disappointed. "Well thanks for coming—"

"I'm sorry, I really have to go," Sierra said, already walking out the door. "I'm going to be late!"

"I guess I'll see you later," Steve called back.

Sierra rushed off without a backward glance. She was still flustered when she got to her car. She couldn't remember the last time she'd enjoyed a meal with a man that much. Had she ever? She was glad of the excuse of having to go; now that she was safely away from Steve, she realized she'd left hurriedly more out of a desire to protect her feelings than any concern about being late for her showing.

She wasn't sure whether she would address these new feelings with Dr. Cayden or not. She didn't really understand them, so she couldn't see herself trying to explain them to someone else.

Chapter 16

Sierra pulled out a beautiful fuschia cashmere sweater to wear with her black skirt and high-heeled black leather boots as she got herself ready for her date with Dale. After her lunch with Steve, she'd shown a house to a very pleasant older woman and finished up some paperwork. However, Steve hadn't left her mind all day. She kept remembering his eyes, how they seemed to bore into her soul. His hands, when he'd reached across the table to touch hers, had been a little rough, but the touch had been gentle.

Sierra shook her head, determined to get her mind to focus. She needed to close on his house and hopefully also close the labyrinth's door that had opened when she met him.

A perfect way to begin to slam the door on her thoughts of Steve was to ready herself for her date with Dale and try her hardest to be as enthusiastic as possible on this date.

By the time Sierra reached the restaurant, Dale was already there. She was informed of this fact by the maître d' at the door, who led her to the table where her date was waiting, sipping water.

The restaurant was dimly lit, allowing the candles that occupied the tables to create an atmosphere of romance. As Sierra approached the table, Dale got up out of his seat to pull her chair out before the maître d' could get there.

Sierra smiled politely. "Thank you."

"I'm happy that we're finally meeting," Dale said. "I've heard nothing but good things about you."

"Same here. And if I hadn't called you back, my mom would have gotten your number and made plans for a date with you herself," Sierra said, laughing.

And just like that, the ice was broken. Conversation flowed easily as they ordered their meals and glasses of red wine. Sierra learned that Dale was a family medicine physician. He explained that he provided comprehensive health care for individuals and families. He talked about his three-year residency at a local hospital. He now had his own practice in a building with a cardiologist and a dentist. He very much liked what he did. That he was also handsome didn't escape Sierra's notice. He was tall, at least six foot four, with broad shoulders and a muscular physique.

During the conversation, Dale revealed that he'd played football in college and had just never lost the desire to wake up early and train. He was the epitome of tall, brown, and handsome, and was very well dressed. He had on a suit that fit him well and that was at home on his body. He looked relaxed and confident. Sierra was attracted to him. And yet throughout the night her mind continued to take long walks back to her time with Steve—something she didn't like one bit.

"Sierra, are you okay?" Dale asked.

Sierra blinked and straightened in her chair as if to adjust her wayward thoughts. "I'm fine, thanks. Sorry."

"I don't mean to bore you with more stories about my family . . ."

Dale had three brothers, one older and two younger, and had been regaling Sierra with stories of their adventures. Sierra actually found the narration funny and was sorry that she was being rude.

"You're not boring me. You guys sound like you have a lot of fun together," Sierra responded honestly, determined to be more attentive.

And for the rest of the date, she *was* more attentive. Dale made it easy, as he was fun and kept the conversation light. Sierra also told him funny stories that had happened to her in real estate and talked about some fun times she'd had in college. He told her how impressed he was that she had her own successful business, and he genuinely seemed to mean it. He even hinted at the power couple they would make together.

By the time the dessert came and Sierra ate a little tiramisu, she was stuffed and happy. This date had been a good idea.

When the waiter brought the check, Dale grabbed it before she could even look at it.

"I'd be happy to . . ." Sierra began.

He gave her a warm smile and shook his head. "It's my pleasure."

He helped her into her coat, and then they walked to the door. She pointed to her car in the parking lot and Dale walked her over to it.

"I had a really nice time," he said as he took her car keys and opened the door for her.

"Me too," Sierra said.

"I think we should do this again."

Sierra smiled. "Me too," she repeated.

"I'll call you," he said. He lightly kissed Sierra's cheek—sweet and chaste—and stepped back to let her get into her car.

Sierra closed her car door and waved at Dale as she drove out of the parking lot. She really liked him: he was very attractive, successful, funny, smart, and a gentleman. He was exactly the type of person that she should be with. He made sense.

When she arrived home, she pulled out her phone and informed Dale via text that she had gotten there safely, per his request. He told her to have a good night and that he'd had a very good time. She wished him the same and again agreed that the evening had been fun.

It had been a good date, and Dale was a good guy. But when Sierra got ready for bed and laid her head down on her pillow, her heart wouldn't behave; it changed the channel in her mind so that the person she thought of before she went to sleep was not Dale but Steve.

Chapter 17

O n the following Friday, after showing some houses earlier in the day, Sierra went to her appointment with Dr. Cayden. She didn't know where they would be headed today. As Sierra took her seat, she looked at the doctor.

Dr. Cayden had her hair in the same severe bun and was wearing the same string of pearls. Her outfit was similar as well. The only thing that had changed were the colors she wore: today she had on a red silk shirt and a khaki-colored pencil skirt. *Maybe the doctor has a uniform,* Sierra thought, amused. Had she done research and found that the silk shirt and pencil skirt were a combination of clothing that immediately put people at ease? Would she wear it every time?

"So, how have you been?" Dr. Cayden asked.

"I've been okay."

"Have you had any dreams this week?"

"No, not really. Not any that I can remember." Sierra knew that she wasn't being truthful; she'd had a wonderful dream. But so much had happened since last weekend that she hadn't had time to digest the events herself, let alone want to share and dissect them. She decided to save those thoughts for another Friday.

"Is there anything that you want to talk about?"

Sierra answered in the negative again.

"All right, Sierra. I'd like to talk about your dreams some more, but first I want to talk about a couple of other things."

Sierra shifted in her seat on the couch, sensing the doctor was about to discuss something serious.

"Do you know what it means to be depressed?" Dr. Cayden asked.

Sierra was a little thrown by the question, though she should have expected it; her other doctor had briefly questioned her about this before referring her to Dr. Cayden, after all. "I would generally guess it to mean that someone is sad all of the time," she said.

"Do you think you know what that would look like?" Dr. Cayden asked.

Sierra only shrugged, not sure if she liked where this was going. Not for the first time, she felt apprehensive in this office. *And this is only visit number two.*

"It can be a condition that causes a persistent feeling of sadness."

Sierra only continued to nod in response.

"It also causes a loss of interest in normal activities. It can manifest, too, as insomnia or excessive sleeping, unhappiness, irritability or frustration over small matters, fatigue, loss of energy, feelings of worthlessness or guilt, and a number of other things that by themselves could mean something else but together turns out to be depression."

"Is that what you're saying is wrong with me? You think I'm depressed?"

Dr. Cayden shook her head. "Not necessarily. But I do

want you to start to really think about your feelings and how often you feel those feelings throughout the day. I will say that you certainly have exhibited several of the symptoms, and I think that you can agree with me on that."

Sierra nodded again, not sure what to say, or if she even wanted to say anything.

Dr. Cayden broke the silence. "I want you to tell me more about your dreams today. You said that you're different characters in the dreams. Tell me about who that person is."

Sierra was still thinking about the idea of her being depressed. She didn't answer.

Dr. Cayden gave her some time, and then prompted her again. "Sierra? Who are you in your dreams?"

Sierra took a deep breath and exhaled slowly. "At first I was a few different women, as I explained before. I was always in a high-stress situation and alone. I was scared in these dreams, to be sure, but I thought about something recently."

"And what was that?"

"In the beginning I was scared and alone, but I never felt like my character in the dreams was someone who would give up easily. It's just a feeling that I had. And then . . ." She paused again, trying to make sense of her own thoughts.

"And then . . ." Dr. Cayden encouraged.

"And then I began to have dreams about me as someone named Dorothy. I mean, my name is Dorothy in the dreams, but I still have my own thoughts, like in all the other dreams."

Dr. Cayden nodded. "Can you describe Dorothy?"

"Like I said, Dorothy seems to be me. I guess I can describe her in terms of how other characters in these dreams seem to perceive her . . ."

"And how would that be?"

"Brave, kind, smart, and caring."

"Can you talk about the dreams in which you are Dorothy?"

Sierra began with the first dream, the one where she met Mary on the bus. She even went on to describe the events that took place after they left the bus. When Sierra got to the very end of the dream, she relayed to Dr. Cayden the thing that really stuck out in her memory: "I was very scared at this point, but the dream didn't end with my being scared. It ended with my thinking about my friend and whether or not she was okay. My concern for her trumped my fear, and I was able to fight through the pain in order to check on her."

Sierra talked about the very next dream and the dream after that, which seemed to be continuations of the first dream as Dorothy. Sierra relayed the details of the jail dream and the dream at the church that ended in the kitchen.

"So, as Dorothy you have these people you care about and that you're learning and growing from," Dr. Cayden said. "These seem to be people with whom you have a goal in common, so you feel a sense of camaraderie with them."

Sierra nodded slowly. "Yes."

"I want to ask you a couple of other questions about these dreams, if you feel comfortable."

Sierra tilted her head. "Sure."

"You said that you prayed in the dream. Do you believe in God, or do you pray not as Sierra but as Dorothy?"

"Yes, I believe in God—though I didn't for a while. And as far as prayer is concerned, I only recently started to pray again . . . after these dreams started."

"Can you tell me what happened to make you not believe in God?"

Sierra instantly looked down and away, and found herself wringing her hands. "Something happened when I was little, and I asked God to help me with it, but he didn't."

Dr. Cayden nodded and let the short silence pass. Then she said, "Do you think you can share with me what you asked God to help you with?"

Sierra wasn't sure she was ready to share this bit of information. Dr. Cayden patiently waited. And then, without even making a conscious decision to do so, Sierra decided to jump off the cliff.

"I was sexually abused as a child," she blurted out, "and during that time I asked God to help me. I prayed every day for it to stop. And it did eventually, but it took a while, and after that I was angry for a long time. Not just at God but at the world."

Sierra stopped talking. She was very proud of herself that she hadn't shed a single tear.

"So you didn't really stop believing in Him," Dr. Cayden said. "You were just angry at Him."

Sierra shrugged. "I don't know. I guess."

Dr. Cayden waited. When Sierra didn't offer anything else, she asked, "What about John? The man at the end of the last dream? Is he someone you know? Maybe someone you've seen before in your real life?"

"He's not someone I physically recognize, but I get the sense that I've somehow known him before."

"And the other people—this Mary and Miss Patty—are they people you know, or do you just have a feeling of familiarity with them as well?"

"I don't recognize them physically either, but I feel as if we have some connection."

"In these last dreams, even though the first two were violent, somehow you weren't as scared as you were in that first couple of dreams. In fact, in the dream in the jail, you seemed to be able to take charge and be somewhat of a leader. Would you agree with that?"

Sierra thought about that for a second, and finally nodded. "I guess you could say that."

"Do you know why that is?"

"In the dream, Mary said I was the brave one," Sierra said slowly. "Maybe that had an effect on me. Everyone around me was doing these courageous things, so rising above the fear felt natural. They all had so much faith that maybe some seeped into me."

"And you don't think that it could have been the other way around?"

Sierra's brows drew together. "What do you mean?"

"I mean, maybe they were borrowing faith and courage from *you*."

The thought had never occurred to Sierra.

Their time was almost up. Dr. Cayden looked Sierra in the eyes. "Did you have anything else you wanted to talk about?"

"Well, there is one thing," Sierra shared apprehensively.

"And what is that?"

"After the dream on the bus where I was beaten, I woke up with a bloody nose and a headache. Could that really be just coincidence? I just can't come up with a rational explanation for why that would have happened."

Instead of being shocked, as Sierra expected, Dr. Cayden looked thoughtful. "How much do you know about sleepwalking?"

"I've looked up some stuff online," Sierra said. "I have some sense of what it entails."

"It's possible that you hurt yourself while sleepwalking and had no memory of running into something or falling when you woke up."

"But that's not really me. I mean, I remember everything."

"That's true, you remember your dreams. I'm saying possibly you're injuring yourself on walls and floors in your home and have no memory of getting out of your bed or off your couch. I don't want to rule it out."

Sierra thought about it. She was not entirely convinced, but it seemed like a possible explanation. "Maybe you're right."

"Next time you come, we're going to move away from your dreams and talk about your life," Dr. Cayden said. "I want you to be prepared to really be open and share."

Sierra agreed that she would. But after leaving the office and thinking about it some more, she thought she might have just lied to the doctor. She wasn't really sure how much more of her life, past or present, she was ready or willing to share.

Chapter 18

The weekend passed with no new dreams or drama. Sierra spent her Saturday doing chores and painting. Sunday morning, she got up and attended church service with her mother and then went over to her mother's house for dinner. Both Irene and Ron were there, along with Irene's husband and her kids. Normally, that would have made for a stressful situation for Sierra, but surprisingly, everyone got along. She didn't feel as threatened as she usually did. Irene and her mom did ask her about her date with Dale, but took in the story and its details as Sierra told it, without fishing for any other pieces of information. Even Ron seemed to be in good spirits. Sierra left quickly after dinner, not wanting the peace to be broken.

It was soon the next Friday and time for another appointment with Dr. Cayden. She was running a little late that day—the week had been a little hectic, as she was in the middle of three closings, including Steve's—but she managed to get to her appointment only a few minutes late; the doctor was still able to see her.

As soon as Sierra took her seat, Dr. Cayden started in. "So, how have you been?"

This time, she wore a dark blue pantsuit with the same

black heels, Sierra noticed. Her shirt was mint-green cotton. She still looked absolutely pulled together and calm. Apparently Sierra had been wrong: she didn't have a uniform, except maybe for her hair, which was in the same severe bun again.

"I've been okay," she answered.

"Have you had any more problems oversleeping?"

"Not as of late, no."

"Good. I really want to set the focus this visit on your life and not so much on your dreams."

"Okay," Sierra reluctantly conceded. She had tried to mentally prepare herself for this new agenda, but still felt resistant.

"I want to talk about your job first. Tell me a little bit about what you do."

Sierra breathed a sigh of relief. She had no problem talking about her job. She was good at it, and it afforded her a decent living. She was able to be her own boss and even had an employee. Her income allowed her to live in a condo downtown and drive the car she had always wanted. And this was exactly what she told the doctor.

"So you enjoy your work?" Dr. Cayden asked.

"I'm good at it," Sierra said, bobbing her head.

"I know that you're good at it," Dr. Cayden said, "but I want to know if you *like* it."

Sierra shrugged. "I think it's like anything else—some days are harder than others, but I think I like it enough."

"Enough for what?"

"Enough that the pros outweigh the cons."

Dr. Cayden made a note on her pad. "When you were a child, what did you dream of being?"

Sierra thought about the question for moment. "I don't

think I dreamed of becoming anything, career-wise. However, I always liked to draw. I would draw anywhere on anything. I would doodle on the back of my school notebooks, on the wall behind my bed where no one but me could see, and even on my clothes and shoes when I could get away with it."

"And what happened to that desire when you got older?"

"Well, I did take some art classes in college and I really enjoyed them," Sierra remembered fondly. "But I had to be practical. That's why I took the business and management classes—and now, as you can see, I've built a successful career, so obviously I made the right choice."

"Why do you think that art would have been the wrong choice or that somehow you would have been less successful if you had pursued that path?"

"It's rare, I think, that an artist is able to be financially successful and appreciated in her own lifetime. At least that's what history teaches us. I didn't want to wait for another lifetime. I needed to be able to take care of myself—because no one else was going to."

"I see. You say that you're happy doing the real estate work and you also admit to having a passion for drawing and art. Which one do you think makes you the happiest?"

Sierra was caught off guard by this question. Thus far, she had been able to answer the questions presented to her with a sense of confidence, but now she wasn't so sure how to respond. What was the right answer? What was the doctor expecting her to say?

Her reaction must have showed on her face a little, because Dr. Cayden added, "There's no right or wrong answer to this question."

Sierra wanted to believe her but she couldn't. She knew that her answer would reveal something about herself that she had already been struggling with for a while. Something she still wasn't entirely sure she was ready to admit to.

She decided to just lay her cards out on the table to the doctor—and to herself. "I like real estate and I like running my own business. I like that I'm the boss. I really like what real estate has afforded for me. But . . . when I paint I feel like myself. I feel no pretense. My painting feels organic, and because of that, it makes me feel my best version of normal—makes me feel truly happy. So the answer is, maybe painting does make me happier . . . but I don't think that I'm ready to live the life of a struggling artist. I've become accustomed to my lifestyle, and I like it."

Dr. Cayden continued to make notes without comment.

The lack of feedback made Sierra feel defensive. "I know that probably says something awful about my character, but at least I'm being honest."

Dr. Cayden looked up at that. "Sierra, I'm not making any judgments here. That's not my job. My job is to listen and encourage and allow you to work through things yourself. As I stated before, there are no right or wrong answers."

Sierra's face cleared the frown that had been firmly planted on her face, and she relaxed again.

The doctor carried on. "Tell me about your family."

"What do you want to know?"

"Whatever you want to tell me."

So Sierra gave her the spiel about her dad and mom and then Irene and Ron. She told the doctor about what they did for a living and shared that Irene was married with kids.

She gave the order of birth of her siblings, and that was it.

"And do you guys get along?"

"I think we get along just as much as most siblings. I mean, yeah, we fight, but I don't think it's anything out of the ordinary."

"Would you say that you're friends with your siblings?"

Sierra smiled. "I don't know. We're family and we always love each other, but sometimes we're definitely not friends."

"Do you have any people in your life you would call friends?"

"Of course I do. I'm not a weirdo. I made friends in school and in life. I have people I hang out with from time to time." Even as she said it, Sierra was having a hard time remembering the last time she'd hung out with anyone.

"What I want to know, Sierra, is if you had a secret, a really personal secret, who would you share it with?"

Once again, Sierra didn't have an answer. She looked at Dr. Cayden's feet, noting that the right one was currently over the left, and then looked at the painting of the orchid on the wall, hoping for that comforting feeling again. Then, finally, she looked at the clock. The hour was almost up; she was being saved by the proverbial bell.

"Wow, where does the time go? I guess we're done for the day," she said, already gathering her things and preparing to leave.

"We still have a few more minutes left," Dr. Cayden said, stilling Sierra's whirlwind of movement. "There's no hurry."

Sierra slowly placed her handbag by her side and took her seat again. She realized that Dr. Cayden's question had unnerved her, and she wasn't at all clear as to why. She just knew that she wanted to get out of this office and away from the therapist's knowing look.

"Do you have anything else that you'd like to talk about? Anything that's happened since you started coming to these sessions?"

Sierra mulled that question over. No, she absolutely didn't want to talk about the panic attack she'd had in her car after that first visit and what prompted it; nor did she care to talk about her confused feelings about Dale and Steve. Yet these were the main thoughts that had permeated her mind for the last couple of weeks. Sierra decided that she would talk about neither and just tell the good doctor that she felt fine. She would merely grab her things and say her good-byes.

In light of her plan, she was shocked to the core when she found herself instead saying, "I had a small panic attack outside of your office after my first visit. I had a little flash-back to something that happened to me when I was a kid."

"Please go on," Dr. Cayden said.

Sierra covered her mouth after her surprise confession, as if to prevent other words from spilling out. Then she noticed that in spite of having shared such private thoughts with the doctor, her world hadn't ended. In fact, she felt a little relieved. She wasn't sure what was going on, but she went with it.

She started by relating what had happened after the last visit when she got in her car. Then she relayed the story of her time in the attic. She refused to allow herself any emotion; she didn't want to betray herself in front of another person. So when she pictured it this time, she imagined that the child wasn't really her but some other little girl, just as she had done so many other times before. She spoke in the kind of detached voice she might use to tell a story she'd read about, not an event in her own life.

When Sierra was finished, Dr. Cayden asked her how long had it been since she had thought about that experience prior to their first visit.

"Years," Sierra said. "I used to have nightmares about it, but those stopped a while ago."

"Did this happen more than once?"

Sierra's head lowered. "Yes," she said quietly.

"And did you ever get any help? Was the person prosecuted? Did you see a therapist at the time?"

"No," Sierra said without lifting her head. "I never told anyone, and because of that he was never prosecuted and I never went to see a therapist. My parents didn't have any idea."

"If you never told anyone, then how did it end?"

Sierra was still looking down. She couldn't bring herself to make eye contact with the doctor. She said nothing.

"Sierra," Dr. Cayden said after a couple of minutes, but Sierra barely registered that she was speaking.

Then she felt a hand on her shoulder, and she almost jumped out of her seat. She looked up and saw Dr. Cayden staring down at her. She felt as if she was waking from a dream.

"Sierra, are you okay?"

She began to adjust her clothes and hair, attempting to fix her appearance into neatness and order. Then she stopped, realizing how absurd she was being. Her appearance hadn't somehow changed in the past few minutes. It was her insides that were full of confusion and turmoil.

"Sierra," Dr. Cayden prompted her.

"Yeah, I mean, yes . . . I'm okay."

"Well, this is good. I think we're making very good progress."

"We are?" Sierra wasn't really convinced.

"Yes, Sierra, I really think we are. I also think that we've done enough work for today."

Sierra felt quite relieved. She was ready to bolt from the office. She knew that she had made a mistake in bringing up those old memories. It was one thing to admit to being molested. It was quite another to dredge up specific memories and let them play in her mind like a horror movie. She had thought talking about Steve would be harder; her feelings for him were in the present and totally alien to her. Now she knew that she had been fooling herself. Refusing to think about something was not the same as being over it.

"I want you to tell me next time if you have any more memories of the molestation, and I also want an update on any dreams that you might have," Dr. Cayden said. "Have you been writing in your diary?" Her voice sounded steady and normal, as if nothing out of the ordinary had occurred.

Sierra nodded.

"Okay, then continue to do that as well, and next time I want you to share some of those thoughts with me, if you feel comfortable."

Sierra was no longer sure that she could answer with anything but nonverbal responses, so that was what she did.

"And, Sierra, we'll have to come back to this subject."

Sierra nodded again. The very thought of it filled her with a complete sense of dread, but she had expected nothing less. She picked up her purse and prepared to leave.

Dr. Cayden smiled at her, put a hand on her shoulder, and squeezed it. Sierra received the comfort without looking at the doctor or even stopping her stride toward the door, because she was on the verge of tears. If she saw any compassion in Dr. Cayden's eyes, she knew she would cry. And she didn't want to cry. Not in front of this woman, not in front of anyone. She couldn't remember the last time she'd done that, and she wasn't about to start now. Tears were a sign of weakness, and she'd vowed a long time ago to always cry in private. She wouldn't break her vow now.

She had already made it to the elevator when she heard Gail, the friendly receptionist, calling to her and asking her about scheduling her next appointment. As the elevator doors opened, Sierra gave a weak nod and wave of her hand indicating her agreement to the time of the next appointment. She breathed a sigh of relief once she was inside the elevator, grateful to be away from Dr. Cayden and her probing questions. But she knew this relief wouldn't last long; what she wanted a reprieve from wasn't her therapist but the memories that she carried with her.

Right now, though, she didn't care to concede that point, so she didn't.

Chapter 19

S ierra got up from her chair by the window and stretched slow and leisurely, giving her back the rest it needed after the arduous two and a half hours of sitting she'd just subjected it to.

Although her mind and body were tired, she felt the best that she could ever remember feeling in a long while. She looked out of her window again and breathed a sigh of contentment. She had a lovely view of the Milwaukee River and the backdrop of Milwaukee's downtown area, but never since she'd moved in had she taken the time to enjoy it. The river held its own beauty in its steady continuity. The river had purpose; it knew what it must do. The canvas in front of her, reflecting the scene outside of the window, stood witness to the appreciation she was finally showing for the world around her.

A little over two weeks had gone by since her date with Dale and her semi-date with Steve. During that time, Dale had called twice to chat and to schedule another date, but Sierra had come up with a number of excuses not to see him again immediately. She needed time to think and understand what she even wanted.

Steve had called as well. He'd left messages on her phone and with Stefani. Sierra couldn't possibly avoid him much longer, as she was still working on closing on the house he was buying. She'd had Stefani draw up the paperwork and set a time for the meeting to take place. She was excited about the sale—and, if she was being honest with herself, she was excited about the prospect of seeing Steve again. *Well, excited and terrified*, she amended. It was a feeling that she was starting to get used to.

The meeting was set for tomorrow, and she was as prepared as she could be. She had closed many times before and usually the process energized her—but this time she just wanted to get it over with so that she could get back to her creations.

She shut out of her mind the fact that she had canceled her appointment with Dr. Cayden for this week and had rescheduled for next week, citing work responsibilities—which was sort of true. But it wasn't the only reason she'd canceled. A lot had been revealed on that last visit, and Sierra was trying really hard not to think about some of those things. She didn't feel ready, not yet. Even though she was the one who'd blurted out the information, she still didn't understand why.

She had, however, felt more than ready to start painting again. In fact, ever since she'd bought the supplies and began to paint again, she simply couldn't stop. As soon as she dipped her paintbrush into the oil and pressed it against the canvas, she felt as if the brush and her heart were connected, and the paintings flowed. She'd started with simple things, like painting a vase filled with daisies sitting on the living room table, and had now transitioned into creating paintings of her family, places she'd visited, and even images stuck in her mind from her dreams. She simply couldn't stop—and she didn't want to. She felt free and that feeling was so pleasant and peaceful that she felt as though she would do anything to keep it.

She yawned and stretched again, then went to the kitchen to make coffee. She'd been so busy painting that she'd barely slept. She didn't want to. Her present was so rewarding that she wasn't even worried about her future and had stopped thinking about her past.

Just then the phone rang. Sierra checked the name: Irene.

"Hello," she said.

"Hello, yourself," Irene responded. "So, you do know how to pick up the phone. I was beginning to wonder."

"Ha, ha, very funny."

"Seriously, I'm a little hurt that you haven't been returning my phone calls. I had to hear about how you've been through Mom. What's up with that?"

Sierra smiled. She had only responded to her mother's calls because she didn't want her calling the police or 911 because Sierra wasn't picking up the phone. Sierra wouldn't put it past her.

"Nothing is up with it. I just haven't had the chance to call you back yet. I've been busy."

Even as Sierra said the words, she knew they weren't true. She'd been dreading having to answer her sister's questions about Dale—and about Steve. She'd called Irene to try and sort out her feelings after her lunch with him.

Irene had thought the situation was both funny and ob-

vious and said, "When was the last time that you were genuinely attracted to a guy?"—which Sierra had no real answer
to, as she couldn't remember ever having felt this way before.
She had liked guys in the past, but this felt like a punch in the
gut. And that was what she'd told Irene.

"Uh-oh," Irene said. "You might be in trouble. This is
someone who got under your defenses and barely lifted a
finger."

Sierra hadn't liked the way that sounded then and she still
didn't now. She had her defenses up for a reason, and no way
anyone would get underneath them.

Sierra was pulled back to her current conversation when
Irene asked, "So, do you think you like Dale better than you
like Steve?"

That was the question Sierra had been afraid Irene would
ask, and she definitely wasn't prepared to answer it. If she
answered honestly, she would incriminate herself. She knew
that she liked Steve more, but she had no explanation as to
why. They hadn't even gone out on a proper date. However,
when she was with him, her heart did somersaults—and yet
he also seemed like an old, familiar friend.

She replied with the only response that she had in her
arsenal: "Why would I like Steve more? Steve and I aren't
dating. That makes no sense."

Irene only paused for a second before saying, "That really
doesn't answer the question."

Sierra didn't respond, and Irene took the hint.

"Listen, don't forget about family dinner on Sunday," she
said. "There's no excuse to miss it."

Sierra knew the entire family would draw the same conclusion, so she resigned herself to attending. The two sisters shared a few more words of small talk before ending the call.

"I love you," Irene said. "Always will."

This was something Irene said often, and although Sierra never said so, it brought her a sense of comfort.

"I love you too," she admitted. She was smiling as she hung up the phone.

She actually felt pretty good still, she realized. As she began to add sugar and cream to her coffee, another image came bursting into her consciousness, and she knew that she had to paint again, right away. She brought the coffee over to the window and set it down on a nearby table before putting a new canvas on her easel. The image radiating from her spirit began to take life through her fingers as she picked up her paintbrush, dipped it in paint, and began to move it along the canvas. Today would be another good day.

Chapter 20

Sierra set off on Friday morning for her office—a small, elegant space around the corner from her condo that she'd been leasing for two years. She used it to meet with clients and handle paperwork and meetings, but didn't require anyone to be there at all times. Stefani went in at least three days a week, and Sierra went in whenever she needed to. Calls to the office when neither she nor Stefani was there were forwarded to both women's cell phones.

She had begun to lighten her workload in the past week, and to commit more energy to her art. She wasn't sure where it was going; she only knew that the transition was exciting and she felt good. But more than that, the change felt right.

Stefani, like Irene, was a wife and mother and had jumped at the opportunity to be able to work out of her home as a secretary for Sierra a few days a week. The arrangement had worked out well for both women.

As Sierra drove, she tried to mentally prepare herself to see Steve again. She wanted to be as professional as possible, but it was getting harder with each day that went by, because each day she thought of him more and more. For some reason, after her dream of John, her thoughts of Steve had intensified tenfold. But just thinking of him wasn't what bothered her; the trouble was that she had a physical reaction to every thought of him.

Her heartbeat and breath quickened now, and she started to perspire. She was afraid that if she did these things just thinking of him, actually being with him would inspire even more embarrassing reactions. Nevertheless, this meeting had to happen. She wanted it to happen. The sooner they closed, the sooner they could part from one another. And even though the thought of that filled her with great sadness, she felt that for the sake of her sanity, she needed it to happen.

As she pulled up to the office, she comforted herself with the knowledge that both Stefani and the sellers, as well as their real estate agent, would be at the meeting. She would have plenty to distract her. She could do this.

She got out of the car and noticed Stefani's car already parked on the street. She opened the door to the office and went in, allowing the light yellow of the walls to help calm her spirit—the reason for the color choice to begin with.

The coffee maker in the corner of the room was already at work, and the smell permeated the office. Stefani was seated at one of the two black executive desks toward the back of the office, identical but for the pictures that occupied the top of each desk. Stefani's desk displayed pictures of her husband and kids. Sierra's desk displayed an old photo of her, her siblings, and their parents. It was taken when she was about five years old and was one of her favorites. They all looked genuinely happy in the picture, and that in turn made her happy. Aside from the family portrait, a print from an artist well-known for capturing African American life experiences and a desk lamp of brushed steel with an adjustable head were the only other items on her desktop.

As Sierra put down her bag, Stefani brought over a cup of coffee—the way Sierra liked it, with a little cream—and then began to brief her about the details of the meeting. Sierra listened respectfully, but she had already gone over the details in her head more than a million times in the last couple of days. She was determined for everything to go well. No matter what, she still prided herself on being the best at whatever she did, and this was no different, regardless of her personal feelings.

"So, I've got the copies of everything together and bottled water and coffee ready to go," Stefani told Sierra. "I also called everyone this morning to confirm the meeting, and they should be here in the next thirty minutes."

"Great, thank you!" Sierra said. She slid into her seat and began to review the documents.

An unexpected hand on her shoulder startled her out of her concentration ten minutes later.

"I'm so sorry," Stefani immediately said. "I just . . . wanted to make sure that you're okay."

"Of course I am, why wouldn't I be?" Sierra asked, puzzled.

"It's just that you haven't exactly been yourself lately. You haven't been really researching any new prospects or showing your usual interest in the ones we have—and I'm worried about you, that's all."

Sierra was about to answer emphatically that she was fine and for Stefani not to worry when she looked up and saw the real concern—and distress—in Stefani's eyes. She knew that she should be completely honest with her; she was not only a great employee, she also tried to be a good friend. She deserved the truth.

"I'm fine," Sierra said slowly. "I really am. I just need a little time to figure out some things. Whatever the outcome is, I'll make sure that I take care of you. You don't have to worry, okay?"

"Okay," Stefani said, relief evident on her face. "And thank you. Thank you for everything."

Sierra smiled and nodded. "Thank *you* for everything."

The next ten minutes passed uneventfully, and then the little bell on the door rang, indicating that the parties were starting to arrive. One by one, the sellers, their lawyer, and their agent entered and were shown to the amber wood conference table surrounded by plush executive chairs in mahogany. Steve's lawyer, a younger man with blond hair, a quick smile, and a matter-of-fact manner, entered just a minute or two later.

The sellers were a young couple with two children; now the wife was pregnant with a third, and they said they had outgrown the house, as they planned for their family to continue to grow. Their real estate agent was an older gentleman with a kind disposition. He and Sierra had spoken on the phone several times, and by this time were fairly comfortable with one another. The two of them chatted as the couple's lawyer, a young woman with auburn hair in a navy blue pantsuit, looked over the documents Sierra handed her.

Five minutes later, Steve walked in the door. Sierra steadied herself, determined to act in a normal manner. She watched as Stefani took his coat and ushered him to the table.

Steve greeted the whole table, but Sierra could feel his eyes on her even as she looked down at her papers.

For the rest of the meeting, in between the signing and reading, she did her best to smile and put everyone at ease. She also tried her best not to look at Steve too long when she addressed him. She kept everything light and easy.

Finally, the deal was done. Everyone left the office relatively quickly afterward—except for Steve, who struck up a conversation with Stefani. Five minutes passed as they talked about Stefani's son, who was apparently on an intramural basketball team that Steve coached. They had a game this afternoon, and both Steve and Stefani were going.

For a moment, Sierra was a little piqued that Stefani hadn't said anything about this personal connection to Steve before now. *But then again, why would she?* she reminded herself. She had never before shown interest in a client's personal affairs. Why would Stefani think Steve would be an exception?

Rationally, Sierra knew this, but the way that they were laughing and talking about the kids on the team made something in Sierra's chest hurt. She wasn't sure what the feeling was, but she was suspicious that it might be jealousy—an emotion she didn't want anything to do with, especially as it related to Steve. She began to gather her personal belongings, trying to leave as quickly as possible.

"Well, Steve, I want to thank you again for your business," she said as she slid her purse strap over her shoulder. "I hope you enjoy your new home." She held her hand out for Steve to shake.

Steve paused in conversation and turned all of his attention, including his infectious smile, on Sierra. She felt her cheeks grow hot, and wished she wasn't so affected by him. She felt her lips turn up even wider in reaction.

Then Steve took her hand, and the smile faded. There it was. That feeling, that response that she experienced every time they touched. To Sierra's horror, it wasn't a fluke.

"No, thank *you*," Steve said. "I appreciate all that you've done. You've been a big help."

Once again, Sierra found herself letting go of his hand first and breaking the eye contact with the pretense of needing to find something in her purse. She hoped that he would get the message, but he didn't seem to be in any particular hurry. She glanced back up at his eyes again and saw amusement. She was annoyed that he had read her again and struggled not to let her irritation show.

"You know, if you don't have any big plans for this afternoon, I would love for you to come to the game," Steve said.

Sierra only needed a second to realize that he was talking to her, because of course Stefani was already going. Before she could come up with a really good excuse not to go, he added, "I mean, I'm sure Stefani would love for you to come too."

Sierra looked at Stefani, and saw that she actually seemed excited about the idea. Sierra thought about all of the times her assistant had gone out of her way to make something happen for her—and all the invitations Stefani had extended for Sierra to come to one of her kids' sports games or recitals. Sierra had always been too busy to go, but today she had no good reason to say no. She sighed. "What time is the game?"

Steve smiled as if he had won a major battle—and maybe he had, Sierra realized. "One o'clock," he said.

"So you'll come?" Stefani asked, her voice full of excitement.

Sierra heard herself say "sure" before she fully understood what was happening.

Spending more time with Steve went directly against everything Sierra's brain had been telling her for the past few weeks. But as she watched him pick up his things and head out the door, she had to acknowledge that her heart didn't mind at all.

Chapter 21

The game was at the middle school, where Stefani's son, Malik, went to school. Sierra was familiar with where it was; she had gone to public schools all her life, and the extra-curricular activities she'd been involved with had taken her to schools all over the city—this one included.

"Do you want a ride to the game?" Stefani asked as they walked out of the office. "We could stop for a coffee on the way there, and I can bring you back here after."

"No thanks," Sierra said. "I have other things I need to do later and might have to leave the game early." She was lying. The truth was, she really needed time to compose her spirit and prepare herself to watch Steve for a couple of hours while still feigning indifference.

Sierra took the downtime between the meeting and the game to grab groceries and pick up some dry cleaning. She then dropped those things off at her home and changed into some-thing more comfortable—jeans, red sweater, and a black leather jacket. She added a leopard-print scarf at the last second. She'd been doing that a lot lately: adding little accessories to her wardrobe that were fun. It made her feel more like she was expressing herself.

She headed to the school feeling pretty confident in what she looked like, and in her ability to be fun and supportive with Stefani while still maintaining her aloofness toward Steve.

When she arrived at the school, she parked in the lot and headed to the entrance, where Stefani had just texted she was waiting for her. The two women chatted amicably as they proceeded to the gym.

Before they walked into the gym, Sierra heard the screech of shoes on the wood floor and the murmurs of the crowd—and then they walked through the door, and the smell of rubber, sweat, and stuffiness washed over her, taking her back to elementary school gym class. She smiled at the memory fondly.

A good-looking gentleman waved his hand at Sierra and Stefani—*Stefani's husband*, Sierra reminded herself. *Devon*. She had met him a couple of times when she had stopped by Stefani's house to drop off or pick up documents over the last two years, but had never spent any time with him in a social capacity.

The two women walked up the bleachers, careful not to step on the various arms, legs, and heads of supporters who were already seated as they made their way to where Devon was sitting with their daughter, Maya.

Devon greeted Sierra with a smile and a friendly handshake and then kissed Stefani. He took her hand as she sat down next to him. The gesture touched Sierra; they had been married for over ten years, and seeing that they were still warm toward each other and seemingly still in love was encouraging.

Sierra began to think about her sister and her husband. They had been married for twelve years and had three children. Blake, the oldest son, was eleven. Taylor, their only daughter, was eight. Their youngest child, Jaylon, was five. Every time Sierra was around the entire family, she felt the love and peace that Irene and Jason had established in their family. But she knew that their path hadn't been an easy one. Many times over the years, Irene had vented and shared arguments and frustrations that had flared up between her and Jason. Sierra, being four years younger and not the best at relationships, didn't necessarily always have a lot to share, but she strived to be a good listener. In doing that, she had actually learned a lot over the years about how to sustain a healthy relationship.

Sierra realized in that moment just how many people she knew who were happy in their long-term relationships. Yet those examples had never stopped her from being scared of her own possible relationships failing. After all, Stefani and Irene were different types of women than Sierra, and they'd had different life experiences. Sierra had always felt that she was a little unusual, maybe even a little crazy, and she couldn't see herself sharing all of who she was with a man. In her heart, she didn't believe that any man would still love her after knowing her completely—so she had never even tried. Did that make her a coward? Sierra flinched at the thought. She'd never thought of herself in those terms before.

She had needed courage to leave home and go to college. She had needed courage to leave her well-paid advertising job, take more classes, and open her own real estate business. She had needed courage to buy her own condo and hire someone to work for her. Those things had all felt courageous at the time, anyway. But even in those cases, maybe she had taken the way that to her seemed safe.

And when it came to relationships, well . . . she had never really fully opened up to anyone. And she still wasn't sure if she really wanted to.

A loud buzzer went off, signaling the start of the game and bringing Sierra back to the present. The kids gathered in the center of the court to jump for the ball and begin the game.

Even with all the activity going on in the center of the court, Sierra's eyes instantly found Steve. He was standing on the sidelines, holding papers and a clipboard. He had changed clothes as well: he was now wearing a blue-and-white track suit that matched the colors of his team's uniform, and had a whistle hanging from his neck. He also had a very serious look on his face as he concentrated on the game.

Another whistle blew, and the kids jumped up in the air for the ball. Steve's team won possession, and the game began.

Sierra was easily able to follow the game, as she was a fan of basketball on both the college and professional level. She cheered on Malik and his team but found herself mostly staring at Steve. He was very impressive as a coach. The kids clearly respected him: they intently listened to his directives. They were also winning. This was something Steve was good at.

The game went on, and Sierra continued to be mesmerized by the way that Steve moved and directed and listened. At one point, he glanced over at the crowd and saw Sierra watching him. A smile spread across his face, and he returned her gaze for a moment—a second that, to Sierra, felt like an hour. He turned his head back around to focus on the game, and Sierra felt her heart catch.

Stefani nudged her. "What was that about?" she whispered.

Sierra straightened her shoulders and tried to act as if she had no idea what Stefani was talking about. "What do you mean?"

Stefani wasn't deterred. "I mean, why is Steve looking at you like he's starving and you're his next meal?"

Sierra laughed at the analogy and then shrugged. "I have no idea."

"Oh, no?" Stefani questioned. But she didn't press her any further.

The buzzer sounded, signaling the end of the game. As the bleachers began to clear out with parents and supporters either leaving or going down to collect their kid, Stefani and Devon kept up happy chatter. Together, their little group walked down the bleachers to meet Malik on the sidelines.

Sierra talked to Malik and the other boys while trying not to make eye contact with Steve. She knew that she should leave now, and yet her body seemed glued to the spot as if by its own volition. It wanted to stay close to Steve.

She felt a warm hand touch her arm. "So, you had a good time," Steve offered.

Sierra nodded. "I did."

"We're going to head out," Stefani called out just then. "Do you want to walk out with us, Sierra?"

Just as Sierra was about to say yes, she felt that touch on her arm again, and those eyes that had been haunting her thoughts called her back.

"Do you think I can talk to you for a second?" Steve asked.

Before Sierra could even think about answering, Stefani answered for her. "Sure you can. We'll catch you guys later." She passed a conspiratorial look to Steve before turning away.

Sierra should have been upset, but she found herself amused again—at Stefani's perceptiveness, and at the fact that she wanted to try and play matchmaker.

Sierra waved good-bye and watched Stefani and her family walk out so that she could look at something to steady herself before facing Steve.

When she looked at Steve again, he was watching her. They looked at each other for a full minute, and Sierra didn't turn away this time; instead, she allowed the excitement that was always ignited by his nearness to flow through her.

Steve smiled the way he always did. "I'm really glad you came. Thank you."

"You're welcome," Sierra said, unable to come up with anything else to say.

Steve's gaze moved away from her eyes, and he looked her up and down from head to feet. "You look good."

Sierra tried her hardest to have no reaction to his compliment but couldn't stop the smile that spread across her face. "Thank you."

"I was wondering what you were doing with the rest of your day," Steve continued.

"Why?" Sierra was immediately suspicious.

"Well, I was thinking that we could spend it together."

She automatically began to shake her head in the negative. "That's not a good idea."

Steve wasn't deterred. "Why isn't it a good idea?"

"I already told you," Sierra reminded him.

"You said that you don't date clients. I'm no longer your client, so that no longer applies."

Sierra hated that he was making sense, as she now had to come up with another reason for them not to spend time together. At least, that's what her head was telling her. But she wasn't so sure anymore if her head was running the show.

"So?" Steve solicited playfully.

"So, what?"

"So, will you spend the rest of the day with me?" Steve asked. He took her hand and linked their fingers together. When she let him, he pulled her just a little closer to him. "Come on, you know you want to," he said softly.

And the truth was, she did. She really, really wanted to. She remembered her thoughts from earlier, when she had been questioning her bravery in relationships. Would she be brave now? She was becoming someone new—and she wasn't sure of who that was, but she knew that she was brave. She was the kind of person who rode freedom buses and spent time in jail for what she believed in. She was daring.

Smiling, with boldness in her spirit, Sierra said, "Okay, let's go."

Chapter 22

They ended up deciding to go have a bite to eat at a steak house Steve suggested. He wanted to drive them there, but Sierra, still on guard, decided that she wanted to take her own car. So they set off from the school with Sierra following Steve.

The steak house was only fifteen minutes away. When they pulled into the parking lot, Steve waved for Sierra to take the first space, closest to the door, and found another one for himself a bit farther away. Before Sierra could get out of her car, Steve was already opening her door for her. He waited for her to get out and set the alarm; he then placed his hand on the small of her back and led her to the entrance. The sensation of his hand on her back made Sierra feel both cherished and safe at the same time.

The restaurant was just ending its lunch service and shifting to dinner, so it was relatively empty; they were immediately escorted to a booth. Seated across from each other with menus in their hands and water placed before them, they both picked up the menus and started to scan, leaving the table in silence. Sierra's heart was beating a rapid drumbeat, a rhythm of exhilaration and trepidation.

CRQ

Steve knew what he wanted to talk about, but he wanted to give Sierra a few minutes to settle in before he started his line of questioning. He was determined to get to the bottom of why she was fighting so hard against the attraction that they so obviously had toward one another. When he was with her, he felt alive and excited, and he was pretty sure she felt something similar. Yet for some reason she didn't seem to want to experience these feelings. He wanted her to be just as excited about this attraction as he was, and if he could do anything to make her more comfortable, he would.

The waiter came back shortly and took their orders. They both ordered iced tea , and filet mignon with potatoes and green beans. The only place they differed was on the potatoes: she asked for hers baked, while he ordered his au gratin.

"I'll bring bread as soon as I place the orders," the waiter promised before disappearing.

Steve watched Sierra slowly sip her water.

"So . . ." he started.

"So . . ." Sierra repeated.

He smiled and began to ease into the conversation. "So, you had a good time at the game?"

"I told you that I did."

"Do you follow basketball in general?"

"Yeah, I like NBA and college tournaments."

"Did you ever play?"

"No. I've never been all that athletic. I'm usually just an athletic supporter."

Steve smiled. "Do you like to work out?

"I try to take walks regularly and go to the gym occasionally, but it's not something I do on a consistent basis," she admitted. "How about you? Do you work out?"

"Hey, I'm a coach, so I try to set a good example and work out whenever I can," Steve said. "That usually means that I'm working out at least three or four times a week."

Sierra smiled. "That's impressive."

"So are you," Steve responded. He took his gaze from her eyes for the first time and let it roam over her. "You certainly look like you work out."

Sierra's face flushed a little, but she merely nodded in response.

Seeing her physical reaction to his compliment, Steve thought this would be a good time to press her about their attraction. "You know, it's okay to like it when I give you a compliment and to express that."

Sierra frowned. "I know it's okay to like a compliment and express that. I don't need your permission."

Steve smiled. At least he had ignited a heated response; he didn't really mind that it was negative, as long as she was allowing her passion to shine through. "Okay, I got it," he said, putting his hands in the air as if surrendering. "I've been put in my place."

This time, Sierra smiled and visibly relaxed.

Steve was relieved that he seemed to be succeeding in putting her at ease and diffusing her hostility. He picked up the glass of iced tea the waiter had just dropped off and took a sip, noting that Sierra was watching him. Then he put the glass down and took her hand, which was lying on the table playing with the corner of her napkin.

"Do you know that it's okay to like me?"

"No, I don't know that," Sierra responded.

Steve felt his whole body go tense with disappointment. "Why do you feel that it's not okay?"

"I don't think I know you well enough yet."

Steve relaxed again, feeling hope return. Whatever this was, he felt confident that she would give it a chance. "You said 'yet,'" he noted.

"Yes I did."

They smiled at each other, and he gave her hand another squeeze before letting it go and making space for the waiter to put their entrees on the table.

"So, how long have you been coaching?" Sierra inquired after swallowing her first bite of steak.

"I've been doing it as long as I've been teaching—almost ten years now. The elementary school where I was working needed a coach for the intramural team and kind of asked the staff to see who would be interested. I've always liked basketball and used to play in high school and college, so it seemed like a good fit. I really like coaching. I feel as though it's part of who I am . . ."

⁓

Sierra listened to Steve intently, liking him more and more as he spoke about his love of coaching and teaching. Passion dripped from his voice when he spoke of inspiring new generations and continuing to fight the good fight in education, even though the system and times in which he now taught made it continually harder and harder to maintain a level of enthusiasm. Between sometimes-apathetic students and parents, tighter and tighter restrictions on school curriculums, and the importance placed on tests, teaching was tough.

"How do you maintain your motivation, then?" she asked.

Steve shrugged. "I know that this is what I was born to do. And every time I'm teaching and coaching, I get an affirmation of that in my spirit. It makes me happy."

Sierra felt a little envious of his sureness for a moment. But the feeling passed quickly, and was immediately replaced by a sense of happiness for him. He was so confident about his purpose; she found hope in his confidence.

"So, what about you?" Steve raised his eyebrows.

"What about me?"

"What makes you happiest—selling real estate or painting?"

Sierra was taken aback at his question, but only for a second. *I'm the one who told him how much I love painting*, she reminded herself. For some reason, she had allowed the truth to escape out of her spirit and through her lips. But then, doing so was starting to get easier for her.

"I guess the answer to that would be painting," she said—and saying it out loud, she automatically felt an easiness come over her. She knew that she had just released something important into existence, and though sharing something so true made her feel vulnerable and scared, she was able to let that go and simply feel good about sharing it.

"So why aren't you doing anything more artistic on a full-time basis?" Steve asked earnestly.

"I don't know why," Sierra said, and then she changed the subject. She'd made enough personal revelations for one day. For now, she just wanted to enjoy the rest of the meal.

Steve clearly saw that she was evading elaborating on the question, but he let her move on to other topics without protest. He didn't press her any further.

They both continued to eat and fell into a companionable silence. They were having a good time. The food was good. The company was good.

Sierra was still perplexed as to how Steve could make her feel relaxed with his conversation and then make every fiber in her being stand at attention when she looked at him. The dichotomy of the two feelings left her in constant confusion about how she felt about him. Even with her heart tugging toward him and her resolve to be brave, she could still sense a wavering inside her—a desire to run from this unknown.

She could never really remember having sustained happiness for long periods of time. The joy and excitement that being with Steve brought couldn't possibly lead to a happy ending—at least, that was where her mind was going now as they finished up their meal. She knew she was thinking too much, and yet having that knowledge didn't stop the thoughts from flowing.

The waiter came and placed the check next to Steve's water glass. Sierra looked at it and Steve looked at her, his gaze daring her to reach for it. Sierra threw up her hands, echoing his earlier gesture of mock surrender, and Steve took his wallet out and paid for the meal. After only a few moments, the waiter was back to pick up the check, and Sierra and Steve both shared a laugh at the speed with which he retrieved Steve's credit card.

"So, now what?" Steve asked after their mutual guffaw was over and he had signed the receipt.

"What do you mean?"

"I mean, what are you doing with the rest of your day?"

Sierra's heart did another flip at the knowledge that Steve desired more of her time. But she also knew that she had already promised Dale she would go to the movies with him that night. The idea that perhaps she was being dishonest by agreeing to go out with Steve even though she was technically already dating Dale gave her pause, but she dismissed the thought; at this point in time, no one had agreed to exclusivity. *This is just an innocent early dinner date*, she reasoned, even as the hairs standing up on her arm while Steve helped her put on her coat said something different.

"Well?" Steve asked when she still didn't answer.

"I have plans tonight," Sierra responded honestly.

"Are you seeing anybody?" Steve asked, his voice suddenly a little less warm.

"Yes, I'm seeing someone," Sierra said. She might as well be clear.

"Oh," Steve said, betraying no reaction. He opened the front door for her and ushered her through. "How long have you guys been dating?"

Sierra didn't answer until they were standing at her car door. "We actually just started dating," she said as she pulled out her keys. "We've been out once."

"Well, I want to see you too," Steve said. He took Sierra's hands into his own and kissed her fingers softly, one by one.

Sierra's heart rate went up, and she could feel her breath quickening. "Umm, you mean tonight?" she asked, suddenly fuzzy. Every time Steve touched her she found focusing difficult.

"It doesn't have to be tonight," Steve said. "I'll take today as enough for today. But I do want to see you again, and again, and again."

Sierra shook her head, hoping to clear her thoughts and be able to give attention to something other than the touch of Steve's lips against her skin. "I don't know about that," she said. But even she knew that her response wasn't plausible. The attraction between the two of them was undeniable. She wanted to see him again as much as she needed her next breath for life.

Steve seemed to read what her eyes were saying as she gazed at his lips. He leaned down, and Sierra went up on her toes to meet him. Their mouths met in the middle, and as they came together, Sierra really couldn't remember ever having experienced anything more wonderful.

The kiss was short and chaste, but then she felt Steve's arms come around her, pulling her toward him and away from the car, and she didn't stop him as he held her in his arms. Something in his embrace was so familiar, even in its uniqueness. She had known him before, somehow.

Maybe in another life, she thought.

He held her in his arms for several seconds that felt like an eternity. Eventually, Sierra remembered where they were—a parking lot outside a restaurant—and began to pull away. As she separated herself from Steve, she suddenly felt cold. She recognized that it probably had very little to do with the temperature outside.

Steve's gaze was steady, and he refused to let her totally disconnect by breaking eye contact. "Sierra . . ." he started.

Just her name on his lips made Sierra want to say yes to whatever was coming next.

"Sierra," he said again, "I like you. I want to see you. It doesn't have to be anything official. I just want to spend time with you. I think we both deserve to see where this goes."

Sierra had to admit that what Steve said made sense. Anyway, who was she kidding? She wanted to spend time with him too.

"Okay," she said, her voice shaky. She let him take her keys and unlock her car for her. He opened her door and helped her into the car. Every touch of his hand was connected to her nerve endings, and her whole body was alert to his very nearness. She could smell his musky cologne; she inhaled as she dipped her head to get into the car, drawing the scent in.

"I'm going to call you later," Steve promised.

"Okay," she said. Steve closed her car door. She knew that he would wait for her to start her car and drive off safely before he walked away. She willed herself not to look back at him through the driver's side window. She put the key into the ignition and then waved at him once more as casually as she could before pulling away and out of the parking lot.

She couldn't remember having said the word "okay" as many times in her whole life as she had in the last twenty-four hours. As she turned the corner and began to make her way back to her condo, she grasped that her "okay" was actually "yes." Just as when she was painting, saying yes to Steve was saying yes to something her heart wanted. For once in her life, her heart would be the leader and her head would simply have to follow.

Chapter 23

ale was a gentleman, just as before. This time he picked up Sierra at her condo. He arrived with a smile on his face and roses in his hand. He was dressed casually, in dark-washed jeans and a pale blue button-down shirt with a black leather jacket on top to keep the chill off of him. He wore nice black leather shoes that looked expensive. His hair was perfectly brushed so that the waves in his short cut flowed impeccably. His skin was just as gorgeous and caramel as the first time she'd seen it. By all measures, Dale was perfect, and Sierra made a note of it.

Sierra herself had on a long, dark gray sweater dress that she'd paired with her tall black suede boots and her red scarf. She had chosen the outfit carefully after getting home from her time with Steve, using obsessing over her outfit for her date as a distraction from her thoughts of Steve. And it had worked, too—right up until Steve texted her saying how much he'd enjoyed their time together and was looking forward to doing it again. Sierra had to admit that she felt the same and texted back "Me too," even as her heart was beating faster simply at reading his text.

Nevertheless, Sierra was determined to give Dale her undivided attention tonight. He was thoughtful, successful, handsome, and kind. On paper, he checked off on every characteristic Sierra was looking for. He deserved a chance, and Sierra was going to give him one.

The drive over to the movie theater took place in awkward silence at first. They appeared to have covered most of their common interests on the first date. Only when Sierra asked Dale about his day did conversation begin to fill the stillness. He was happy to talk about some of the more interesting points of the day—without naming any names, of course. Sierra happily let him take over the talking. For one, he really seemed to enjoy talking about his job, certainly more than she liked to talk about hers. Secondly, with him talking, she could try and concentrate on his words and not allow her mind to drift.

But after he'd shared two short stories, he stopped to ask her how her business was going.

She told him about the sale she'd closed earlier in the day—leaving out the game and dinner that had followed—and he congratulated her with genuine excitement and pride in his voice. He then asked her about other clients and prospects she was working on.

Sierra paused. "Actually, I'm starting to lighten my load."

Dale glanced over at her. "What do you mean?"

"I mean, I'm taking a little more personal time."

Dale nodded in understanding. "Yeah, breaks are good. It's nice to have a little vacation. Afterward, you feel totally rejuvenated and ready to work and focus on the tasks at hand. I know you know with anything, though, you should strike while the iron's hot and people are interested. I believe in rest, but you can't stagnate. Time waits for no man or woman."

Sierra nodded, realizing that his thoughts mimicked her own less than three months ago, but now, she wasn't so sure she wholeheartedly agreed with him, at least not when it came to real estate .

"So, what are you going to do with the free time?"

"I'm going to try and relax, and I've also started to paint again," Sierra said, brightening at the thought of her art.

"Oh, wow," Dale said. "I didn't know you painted. It's really good to have a hobby."

When Dale said the word "hobby," Sierra felt a twinge in her body that told her she was offended by the idea of her painting being a hobby. She knew he didn't mean anything by it, and if she was being honest, that was exactly what her painting was—but still, she couldn't deny that twinge.

When Sierra made no response to his comment, Dale added, "I would really like to see some of your paintings, one day, if you don't mind."

Sierra didn't know if she minded or not, but she appreciated his interest. Her warm feelings toward Dale were renewed.

When they got to the movie theater, he paid for the tickets.

"Do you want anything from the snack bar?" he asked.

She really wasn't hungry at all; in fact, she was still pretty full from her earlier meal. She did, however, like to snack on something when she watched a movie. "How about some Reese's Pieces?" she suggested.

"Coming right up!" Dale said.

A few minutes later, candy delivered, Dale put his hand on the small of Sierra's back—*just like Steve*, she thought—and led her through the movie theater to their show. He confirmed with her where she liked to sit in the movies and then led her to the middle of the auditorium in the middle row. The theater was only halfway full, as the movie had been out for a couple of weeks.

As the movie began, Dale positioned his body so he was as close to Sierra as he could possibly be without invading her personal space. She didn't mind; she felt warm and safe.

The movie was a good one. It was a thriller-suspense and Sierra felt engaged from start to end, although the plot was nothing new. Man works for the CIA, somehow his family's identity is compromised, and the rest of the movie is him trying to keep his family alive while finding out who compromised his position. There were a few moments where Sierra jumped because of the carnage or an explosion, and each time Dale was there to take her hand or put his arm around her shoulders as needed. All in all, she had to say, it was shaping up to be another pretty good date.

She declined Dale's invitation to eat dinner after the movie ended, explaining that she had eaten earlier, but she did agree to go somewhere for a drink or an appetizer.

The place Dale chose was a well-known spot downtown that offered specialty appetizers and live jazz. They each ordered a glass of wine, and Dale ordered small crab cakes and bruschetta. He talked some more about his family and job, and then they both sat back and listened to the music for a while. It was nice.

"Would you like to dance?"

Sierra was startled by the question, as she had been so focused on the music and atmosphere that she'd lost herself for a minute. She didn't particularly want to dance, but she looked over at Dale, who was already offering his hand, and decided that in the interest of fair play, she would give it a try.

She allowed Dale to lead her to the dance floor as the band began to play a slow song. He held her in his arms and moved her gently around the floor. Sierra noted that being in his arms was nice. His touch was tender and nonthreatening, even as he held her close.

After a few minutes, Dale pulled her closer and tightened his hold ever so slightly. Sierra wasn't threatened by his move, but she didn't like it. She knew that if she liked him more, then she would have found the move to be endearing—but as it stood, all she felt was just a little confused.

The song ended, and Dale led her back to their table. They passed another hour full of conversation and laughter, and then mutually decided that it was time to go.

Dale drove her home and walked her to the door. He took her keys and opened the door for her and then gave her a hug and kiss on the cheek. He smiled, and Sierra smiled too. He made sure she closed the door before he walked back to his car.

As soon as she was alone inside her condo, Sierra sighed—not in longing but in frustration and confusion. Dale was really nice, and they had fun together. But Steve made her feel alive. Before today's date, she'd thought she knew what decision to make, but now she wasn't sure of anything. A thought occurred to her suddenly: *I'll pray about it.*

She realized that, lately, her prayer life had come alive

in a way that it hadn't been in a long time. This renewal had begun with the dreams, and more and more since that first dream, she'd found herself talking to God. Sometimes the exchange was in traditional prayer form, but more often than not, she just had conversations with Him. She wanted peace in her life, and lately she had been asking Him about her purpose.

It was through these talks that she'd decided to start painting again and to lighten her workload. Granted, what she heard back wasn't a bellowing voice from the skies but an inner voice speaking back to her—one that sounded a lot like her own voice. But whatever this was, she felt better after she prayed. If praying could help with her dreams and decisions about work, it could certainly help her make a decision about whom to date.

She pushed away from the front door and headed to the bedroom. She had promised her mom she would come to Sunday dinner that weekend, and the thought crossed her mind as she began to remove her clothes. Once again, she would have to mentally prepare. This time, she promised herself, she wouldn't be baited into another argument with her brother, forgetting that the last time they were together there was no argument.

When she was taking off her earrings, she heard her phone buzzing. When she looked at her phone, she realized that she actually had two texts. The first was from Dale, wishing her a good night. The second, from Steve, read, "Here's hoping that you didn't have as good a time with him as you did with me." He then also wished her a good night.

Sierra shook her head and texted them both good night,

promising herself that she would make some decisions soon. She didn't feel comfortable seeing them both, and she knew that if she let Steve know she was dating other people, she also had to let Dale know.

But she didn't want to think about it tonight. It was starting to make her feel a little stressed, and besides, she was exhausted. She finished getting ready for bed and then pulled back the covers and lay down. She was asleep before her head hit the pillow.

Chapter 24

*W*hen she woke up on Sunday morning, Sierra decided to again attend Sunday service at the church her mom had gone to for the last five years, and which Irene also attended. Even Ron went too sometimes.

Sierra had to admit that she had been impressed by the service the previous Sunday; she was willing to give this pastor, Pastor Miller, another shot. According to Sierra's mom, Pastor Miller had managed to triple the size of the congregation in the ten years he had been senior pastor of the church.

Sierra didn't inform her mom and sister that she would attend the service. She wanted to sit in the congregation anonymously and be free to have her own experience without being under the watchful eye of her family. She knew they wanted her to join the church, but she didn't feel ready for that yet.

Sierra put on a black dress with sheer tights, a red blazer, and red boots. It was April now and she could get away with her lighter gray jacket.

She arrived at the church ten minutes early, but the parking lot was already packed, as usual, and even in the large sanctuary—so big that a large screen hung above the pulpit so the people seated in the back could see what was happening up front—the seats were filling up fast. Sierra was lucky to find a seat in the fifth row.

After the initial prayer and greeting came worship music. During this time, Sierra allowed herself to lift her hands and sing. She closed her eyes and could see the jail from her dreams. She remembered the women crying and singing, and tears began to sting her eyes. She took her hand and wiped the tears away, but continued to sing. Just as in the dream, her body swayed back and forth.

The song was familiar. She didn't know all the words, but she didn't let that stop her—she just sang the chorus as it repeated itself. She kept her eyes closed and allowed herself to be carried out of the sanctuary and into another spiritual space. She felt different, but good. When the songs came to an end, she felt someone tap her shoulder; it was the usher, offering her a tissue. Sierra smiled and accepted with thanks.

After one more song and the offering, Pastor Miller got up to preach. After praying, he informed everyone that most of the sermon would come from Hebrews and beckoned the audience to turn to Hebrews 11, starting at verse one.

"'Now faith is the substance of things hoped for, the evidence of things not seen.' The Amplified Bible states that 'Now faith is the assurance (the confirmation, the title deed) of things [we] do not see and the conviction of their reality [faith perceiving as real fact what is not revealed to the senses].' The title of this sermon is Faith, the Courageous Factor."

Amens were given throughout the congregation.

"A lot of people associate faith with a type of feeling," Pastor Miller continued. "When you say 'faith' to a lot of people, they conjure up images of different churches or denominations, and which one makes them comfortable. Usually, whatever religion they grew up with will be the one that they will relate to a faith that puts them at ease." He looked out at the congregation. "I challenge you today to think about faith in a different way. I challenge you to think about faith in a way that might make you uncomfortable. I challenge you to think about faith in terms of truly believing in your dreams coming to pass, the dreams that have not yet manifested themselves in your life."

Sierra saw a few heads nodding around her.

"I realize that if you're here, on some level you may believe in the God whom you can't see. But now I implore you to allow yourself to believe not only in that God but in the dreams that He placed in your heart. Believe that if He placed those dreams inside of you, He has the ability to allow you to see those dreams manifested in your life." He leaned forward on the podium. "Now I know with life looking the way it does these days, it's hard to even allow yourself to hope for the possibility of these things coming to pass. Your circumstances and fear have you in a chokehold, and you feel like you can't breathe or go on sometimes, let alone dare yourself to hope. But that is what God expects of you. You have to believe and have faith in order for God to work in your life."

Sierra listened intently along with the rest of the worshippers. Pastor Miller's words were reaching deep inside her.

"I know it's hard," he went on. "It was hard for all the people who came before you. It was hard for our mothers and fathers to dream and for their mothers and fathers to dream of a better life. But they did dream, and not only that, they fought for those dreams to manifest themselves. They took courage—and faith—into their hands."

Pastor Miller went on to cite the rest of Chapters 11 and 12 of Hebrews, going down the list of people in the Bible who kept their faith in God's promises even though everything in the natural world pointed to the opposite outcome, that negative outcome revealing itself.

"And that's what it's going to take," he said. "It's going to take courage to believe in what you can't see. It's going to take faith and courage to get up and keep trying without any physical evidence that the next try will be any different from what you've already experienced. It's going to take faith and courage to change your life and see a manifestation of your dreams. It's going to take faith and courage to see a manifestation of your destiny, and difficulties will arise as you embark on this journey of faith. But just when it looks like it's over, and life starts to get harder than it's ever been, that's when you'll began to see the manifestation."

Pastor Miller slowly walked around the pulpit, addressing the left, right, and then middle pews as he gazed out at the congregation.

"Life will change and continue to change in ways that you may not at the time understand. Some changes you'll identify as good and some changes you'll identify as bad, but I've come to let you know that all things work to the good of those who love the Lord and are called to His purpose. If you stay in faith, all things will work toward bringing you closer to the dream that God has placed in your heart. But, you have to do the work and be obedient to the direction that God is leading you in, and in order to even know what direction that is, you need to pray."

Sierra took in everything that the pastor said, and she felt exposed. It was as if he was talking directly to her and her circumstances. For the second time that morning, she felt tears starting to come down her face. She immediately wiped them away with the tissue that she'd used earlier.

She was unprepared for this amount of emotion and didn't know what to do with all of these feelings. She sat through the rest of the sermon looking at the big screen instead of at the pulpit for fear of making eye contact with the pastor. She was sure that if she did, he would be able to see that he was talking about her.

With every word of the sermon, Sierra felt that much more bare and raw. She sat as still as she could and tried to get herself under control.

By the end of the sermon, everyone was excited, and they stood and clapped and raised their hands to God, thanking him for the message they'd just received. Sierra held herself still, not sure what to do. She felt a connection to not just the message but God Himself. She knew that He was speaking to her; she just wasn't sure what He wanted her to do.

Pastor Miller gave the invitation to come to Christ and join the church. Sierra felt something move in her spirit and almost got up and joined the others walking to the front of the church. But something else was holding her back. She didn't know what. She allowed the time for the call to invitation to pass, and only relaxed when it did.

As Sierra filed out of the church with everyone else, she

knew that she looked like the same person who'd gone into the service—but she wasn't. She knew enough about the word of God through her experiences in church as a child when she attended with her family, and from growing up under her God-fearing mother's roof, to understand that once you knew the truth, you were responsible for knowing it and acting on it. But she still didn't know if she was ready.

Chapter 25

Sierra got to her mom's house a little after Irene and her family had already arrived. Ron opened the door for her, and after a quick "what's up" he resumed his seat on the couch in the living room, where he was watching the NBA afternoon lineup with Irene's husband, Jason. Jason got up to give her a hug, and then she headed into the kitchen.

The kids, Irene, and Pearl were conversing, playing, and putting the finishing touches on Sunday dinner when Sierra came into the kitchen—but as soon as she walked in, the kids rushed over and she bent to give them hugs and kisses. They were always quite happy to see her and that made her feel good; she felt the same way.

"How you doing?" Irene asked as she gave her a hug.

"I'm good," Sierra replied.

Pearl grabbed her in a bear hug and kissed her.

"Hey Mama," Sierra greeted her, laughing. When her mom released her, she sat down at the kitchen table.

They all did a lot of talking and laughing. Everyone seemed to be at ease and having fun. Sierra liked the way it felt.

Irene looked at Sierra's outfit. "Did you go to service this morning?"

"Yes," Sierra said. "I really enjoyed the sermon."

Irene frowned a little. "I wish you would have told us you were going."

"We could have sat together, like last time," Pearl said, looking a little disappointed as well.

But the two, surprisingly, didn't linger on the subject. They moved on to other topics before Sierra could even respond.

Sierra was taken aback that the subject was closed so quickly and that both her mom and sister seemed to accept her decision without any real argument—that is, until her mom presented her next question: "So . . . how have you and Dale been doing?"

Her mom tried make the question sound benign, but Sierra wasn't fooled. She found that she wasn't angry, though, just amused. That was a different feeling for her.

"We've been doing fine, I guess. We're simply getting to know one another right now."

Pearl beamed a smile and looked as if she was going to move on until Irene said, "And are you and Steve getting to know each other too?"

Sierra shot her sister a look that told her she didn't appreciate the question, but Irene's face held a smile and her eyes were warm, and Sierra knew she had no malicious intent, so she calmed her ruffled feathers and decided to try and not take herself so seriously. "Yes, I'm getting to know Steve too, and that's the end of this conversation."

Sierra's mom immediately chimed in. "Who on earth is Steve?"

Sierra merely shook her head. She wasn't talking.

With amusement in her voice, Irene comforted their mom, saying, "Don't worry about it, I'll tell you later."

Sierra was positive that she would and felt no need thereafter to offer any explanation. She knew they would talk either way, so she decided to accept the situation for what it was and have a good time at this dinner.

When dinner was finally ready, the family blessed the food and sat down to roast, potatoes, and carrots. Pearl encouraged Ron to talk about his new job at the cable company, which he was pretty happy with at the moment; Irene's kids talked about school; and as the dinner continued, Sierra and her siblings began to talk about old times: playing kickball together, car trips down South to visit their now-deceased grandparents, and Christmases when they woke each other up and ran downstairs with excitement to see what gifts would be underneath the Christmas tree. They talked about their fights as well. And they all laughed and had a good time.

The conversation reminded Sierra that although she'd had some pretty bad times in her childhood, she'd also had some very good times—and maybe, just maybe, the good outweighed the bad. She looked around at her family seated at the table and wondered what they would do if they knew what had happened to her. She wondered if they would treat her the same. Would they be angry that she never told? Would they have any reaction at all? Would they believe her? She didn't really know, but for the first time, as she gazed around the table at her loved ones, she wanted them to know. She wanted them to know who she really was.

Chapter 26

Sierra opened her eyes to darkness. She paused for a couple of seconds and closed her eyes again. She then opened them back up and waited for them to adjust. Slowly looking to the right and to the left, she allowed the moon and the stars to illuminate the scene around her and help her to evaluate the situation.

Cypress and willow trees were all about her. Her feet felt heavy and moist. She looked down and realized that she had on heavy boots that were covered in mud. She heard the sounds of different animals and insects moving close by. In the distance, she could see the outline of a large body of murky water. *A swamp*, she thought. *I'm in a swamp.*

She remembered going to sleep after she left her mother's house and surmised that she was dreaming now. She turned in a full circle to try and get a better understanding of what she was doing here, and just as she completed her turn, she felt movement from right behind her. Her heart jumped, and she put her hands up in a defensive stance as two women appeared from out of the darkness.

She had never seen either woman before. They were both dressed as she was, with long, heavy skirts and head wraps and heavy material thrown around their shoulders to fight away the night's chill.

One of the women had a small child tied to her chest. "What's wrong?" she asked. "Why have we stopped? Did you hear something?"

Sierra looked at both women, trying to get a handle on what they were all doing in a swamp in the middle of the night. Both women looked at her expectantly. Sierra was becoming very familiar with the look: it said that Sierra knew the answers. It was the look people always gave her in her dreams. She was finally beginning to believe they were right in trusting her to know the answers.

"You know they're right on our trail," the other woman said. "That's what you said. You said we just had to keep going north and follow that star."

Sierra looked in the sky where the woman was pointing and saw the star, the same star from a dream she'd had before. Only in the last dream she had been alone and had *felt* all alone. Looking back at the women again, she finally put the pieces together. They were runaway slaves and someone was looking for them.

"You said there was no turning back," the one with the child said. "He's going to sale, my baby. And you said that he was going to keep on raping you if we didn't go right now."

That last part got Sierra's attention.

"Are you okay?" the other woman asked.

Sierra looked again at the sky and the stars. She then looked over at the women waiting for her to lead. She turned in the direction of the star and with determined steps moved forward into the night.

Chapter 27

Dear Diary,

Things were going great. I had dinner with the family two Sundays in a row, and they were good days. There was very little fighting. We got along. I closed on two houses, including Steve's house. I've been painting and that has brought a newfound joy into my life that had been missing for some time. My love life has even taken off. I currently have two men interested in me, and although the idea of this fills me with some anxiety, ultimately I'm having some fun.

The thing is, I thought I could just move forward with my life and not go back to the emotions that were riled up in my last therapy session. I had no real bad feelings or thoughts since then and was even thinking that somehow I had forgotten a lot of the horrible details of those events over the years. I thought that maybe, now that I'm desensitized, I could possibly share this with my family. I really thought I would be able to move on ...

Sierra put the journal down on the table. She felt a headache coming on even thinking about the memories that had plagued her since Sunday. This was Wednesday, and almost two weeks had passed since she'd last seen Dr. Cayden. She still didn't feel ready to continue the conversation about the sexual abuse.

She got up from the couch and walked to the window. She looked out at the night sky and watched the moon and stars work together to light the night. Everything worked together so perfectly. The world was in sync. But her mind had once again become chaos.

Sierra could still remember the first time. She closed her eyes and could smell the lingering aroma of the cigarette smoke. The living room was covered with brown and yellow wallpaper. A velvet picture hanging depicted a beautiful young black woman in a flowing yellow dress. An air conditioner held the window open, blowing out cool air and emitting a loud buzzing sound. The couch was a plaid mix of yellow and beige. The record player was playing a popular R&B tune.

Diana's mom had gone out to the store and left Wayne in charge. Even at the young age of five, Sierra was aware of his eyes following her around the room, and she knew something about his gaze wasn't right; it made her uneasy. She tried to focus on the games that she and Diana were playing on the living room floor, but Wayne sat down with them and began to play too. He tickled his cousin playfully, and then he tickled Sierra.

His face held laughter as he watched Sierra laugh and playfully try to move out of his grasp. His hands grazed her behind and it made her feel strange, but everyone was still joking and laughing so she let the uncomfortable feeling subside. Her friend Diana was there; nothing bad could happen with her friend there, could it?

Diana's mother was gone less than thirty minutes. Diana

was having a good time. Sierra was having a good time with her friend. Wayne went and got them freeze pops from the freezer and used his teeth to open the treats. He gave his cousin the red one and then watched as Sierra ate the top piece off the orange one, smiling in a weird way. Sierra took her freeze pop and went and stood next to Diana.

When she was done with her freeze pop, Diana got up to use the bathroom, and Wayne, who was now on the couch, beckoned Sierra to sit on his lap. Something in Sierra's spirit felt uneasy at his invitation, but he was in charge. No one else was there. She slowly walked to the couch and allowed herself to be lifted onto his lap. When she was seated, she instantly felt something hard and uncomfortable underneath her. She wiggled to try and move away from the object that was poking her, but that only seemed to make it worse.

Sierra tried to get down off Wayne's lap, but he wouldn't let her get down, and the more she struggled the more he laughed and held her tighter and closer to him. Sierra began to whimper, starting to panic.

"Shh," Wayne said. "Don't worry. I'm almost done."

Sierra continued to struggle anyway, and then Diana came around the corner. Wayne let her go, and then he got up and left the room.

Sierra moved away from her window in her home. She knew that she wasn't over it—but she now knew that she definitely wanted to be. She had a feeling that whatever power these memories had over her was holding her back. She sat back down on her couch, and as she picked her journal up once more, she made the decision that she would keep her appointment with Dr. Cayden this Friday.

Chapter 28

Sierra arrived in the reception area of Dr. Cayden's office on time, and instead of immediately ushering her into the office, as she had in the past, Gail directed her to a seat in the waiting room.

"Dr. Cayden is still finishing up her last appointment," she explained. "But they'll be done any minute."

Sierra picked up a magazine promising cooking and gardening tips and browsed through it, not really concentrating or seeing the pages but using it to look occupied. Her leg bounced up and down with nervousness. Her palms were sweaty; she wiped them off on her black dress pants so they wouldn't stick to the pages of the magazine.

Gail was just as friendly as she always was as she answered phone calls and took messages. Bored with the magazine, Sierra listened to her and looked around the waiting room, assessing the décor. It was exactly what a typical doctor's office looked like: It had drab beige walls and one row of standard black chairs that were steel with cushioned seats. There was a coffee table filled with magazines, a coffee maker with cups beside it, and a water cooler.

"Are you comfortable?" Gail called over from behind her desk. "Do you need anything?"

"I'm okay," Sierra said. She knew she wasn't okay. But Gail certainly could do nothing to ease that discomfort, so no need to bother her with her woes.

After less than ten minutes, Dr. Cayden's door opened up and a young woman who appeared to be in her early twenties walked out. She was dressed very casually, in sweatpants and a long-sleeved T-shirt. Dr. Cayden sent her over to Gail's desk, then turned her attention to Sierra, smiled, and waved her hand as an invitation for Sierra to enter her office.

❧

"Sierra, it's good to see you. I'm glad you decided to return."

"Thanks," Sierra said, feeling a little guilty. "I'm sorry I had to cancel my appointments before."

"That's fine. I understand work obligations. How is work going for you?"

"It's good. I sold two more houses and picked up a few more clients through referrals." Sierra was happy to talk about work this session. The subject was safe and nonthreatening— well, usually.

Dr. Cayden smiled. "Congratulations! And how's everything else?"

"Everything else is going pretty well. I decided to start painting again and it feels good. I also have been spending more time with my family, and we actually seem to be getting along pretty well, so . . ."

"That's all very good! I'm happy to hear it."

Dr. Cayden made no notes and was very warm and pleasant now. Sierra's tension eased, and she loosened up. She shared the details of her family dinner on Sunday and even began to open up about her dates with Dale.

"Dating sounds healthy," Dr. Cayden said. "Do you like Dale?"

Sierra shrugged, as she always did. "What's not to like?"

"That's not really saying whether you like him or not . . ."

Sierra realized that she was going to have to talk, really talk, in order to make any progress. She couldn't yet understand why she felt so apprehensive about talking about her love life with anyone, but she was beginning to realize that there was no real way around it.

"The thing is . . . The thing is, there's this other guy."

"Aha, and tell me about him."

Sierra told Dr. Cayden how she'd met Steve, and she tried to explain her feelings about him—how she felt both relaxed and uncomfortable around him, how she felt as if maybe she had known him before, in another life. Something about him was so familiar. She described how she thought about him all the time, even when she tried her hardest not to.

"Why would you not want to like him?" Dr. Cayden asked. "Are you afraid of something?"

Sierra threw her hands up in frustration. "That's just it. I don't know. I think he does scare me. I just feel as if I have no control over the situation."

"Maybe that's what scares you."

"Maybe." Sierra nodded.

"Sierra, can I ask you something?"

Sierra nodded again, wondering why she would suddenly ask this now, when she hadn't asked it ever before.

"What's the worst thing that could happen if you trusted your feelings and allowed yourself to like Steve completely?"

Sierra put her head in her hands and rocked back and forth for a few seconds, unexpectedly distressed by the question. After several minutes, she quietly answered, "I guess the worst thing that could happen would be that he leaves me. That he'll get to know me and won't really like who I am. But by then, I'll like him so much that his leaving will crush me."

Dr. Cayden nodded and made a note. "You think that you wouldn't be able to survive that?"

Once again, Sierra shrugged. "I probably could, but what's the point of opening yourself up to that kind of hurt?"

"In order to open yourself up to joy and happiness, you have to open yourself up to the possibility of hurt and have faith and confidence that if—and that's an *if*—that hurt comes, you'll be strong enough to get through it."

Sierra was silent again, taking in the doctor's words, and Dr. Cayden allowed her that space. After several minutes, she very carefully introduced the next topic.

"You know that I have to ask you about the sexual abuse that we began to talk about on the last visit. I told you we would come back to it, and I know that it makes you uncomfortable. Nevertheless, I think it's important for your growth that we address it."

Sierra, with her head down again, nodded in confirmation of the doctor's words. She'd known that it would come back to this. She even knew that this was why she had even showed up to the appointment today. The time had come to talk about it, whether she wanted to or not.

"I asked you before how, if you never told anyone, the abuse stopped. Can you answer that question for me now?"

Sierra nodded. "He was a star athlete, and he got a football scholarship to a school out of state. After he left, it never happened again."

"And why did you never tell your parents, or your family, or any of your friends?"

Sierra, still not looking up, spoke in a monotone, the words flowing out like water through a faucet. "I was scared to tell, because he told me he would hurt my family and because he told me that my parents wouldn't believe me, that it was my fault because I let him."

"How old were you when this happened?"

"About five or six."

"And how long did this go on?"

"For about a year." Sierra felt relief in the release of this trauma that she'd never talked about until now. It was hurting her, and it felt shameful, but it also felt good, like a cleansing.

"And do you think that a child that age is ever at fault if someone who is older, bigger, and stronger than she is manipulates her into sexual abuse?"

Sierra could feel the tears start to form again, but she said nothing.

"Sierra, you were a little girl, and he manipulated you. Can you understand that it was manipulation? Do you understand that it wasn't your fault?"

Sierra couldn't bring herself to speak. The tears started to flow in earnest now.

"Sierra, how did it make you feel when he did what he did?"

Sierra let out a loud sniffle and in an angry voice bellowed, "It made me feel ugly, and dirty, and ashamed."

A crease of concern appeared in Dr. Cayden's brow line. "Is that why you never told anybody? Because you were ashamed and afraid of what they would think of you?"

Sierra nodded silently. "If I told anyone, they would see how dirty and ugly I am. They would think bad things about me."

"Do you think that your family and the people who love you would really think bad things about you if you shared the trauma of what happened to you?"

Sierra nodded. "I think they think bad things about me now."

"What makes you think that?"

Sierra shared how her brother teased her, and how her mom used to always critique her weight and her love life, and how her sister always wanted to know everything about her life and was always trying to give her advice.

"Sierra, I can tell you that it sounds like normal family dynamics. Brothers tease you and sisters give advice. Moms critique and advise. That's what families do—and usually these things are coming from a loving place."

Sierra just sat there.

"I think you should tell your family what happened to you. You don't necessarily have to go into details, but I think it would be a good idea for you to open up to them or at least to one person in your family whom you feel you can confide in. I have a feeling they'll surprise you, in a good way. But again, you need to know that whatever the outcome is, you can handle it and you'll be okay. Holding this inside hasn't helped you. It will continue to eat you up inside if you continue to give it the power to do so."

Dr. Cayden's words began to filter through the mire of negative thoughts packed in Sierra's mind. Could it be true? Would telling her family about what had happened really help her?

"Talking about the abuse tends to take away its power. This is not your shame—and yet it seems to me that it has hindered your relationship with your family and your relationships with the opposite sex, because you're living a life of fear and restraint, hoping that no one will find out your secret. You're fearful of what they might think."

Sierra listened closely to Dr. Cayden's words.

"Do you understand that what he did to you is his shame and not yours? Do you understand that it wasn't your fault? You didn't have the power there—he held it all. Do you understand that? By talking about the abuse and learning to get past it, you can take your power back."

Sierra nodded.

"I'm sorry, Sierra," Dr. Cayden said, her voice firm. "Can I hear you say you understand that what happened to you wasn't your fault?"

Sierra sat still.

"I would like you to acknowledge with your own words that you know that what happened to you wasn't your fault."

Sierra looked up then—not at the doctor but out the window. She thought about the first time she'd come to this office, and her thought that maybe someone could see her from the other building. She whispered, "It wasn't my fault."

"Sierra, can you say it louder? I want you to be convinced that as a little girl, it was impossible for you to be culpable in your own sexual assault. I want you to know that continuing to take blame and to be ashamed allows this person to have power over you. You're not a little girl anymore. You have power. You have a voice. Can you say to me that this wasn't your fault?"

Sierra thought about all that Dr. Cayden was saying. She thought about the years she'd wasted hiding her feelings and hiding what he did to her. She thought about the misery she felt, and how alone and scared she was.

She thought about the dream where she was lost in the forest and couldn't find her way out. She thought about how looking at all the stars and the darkness made her feel so solitary and abandoned. She'd tried to help herself by using the stars to find her way, but that hadn't worked. It seemed to her that she only found her way in her dreams when others were around her. Just as she had in the last dream.

She thought about her life. Had she created a life of loneliness by shutting out the people whom she knew in her heart cared about her?

She knew—somewhere deep inside, she knew—that what he'd done to her wasn't her fault. He'd made that little girl feel as though it was, but this adult Sierra knew better. She knew that it wasn't.

Well, if you know that, then just say it.

With more confidence and a little louder, she said, "It was not my fault."

Dr. Cayden smiled and nodded. "And because you know

it's not your fault, you also know you have nothing to be ashamed of. Can you tell me that you're not ashamed?"

Sierra looked straight at her. "I'm not ashamed."

Dr. Cayden smiled again. "And since you have nothing to be ashamed of, you also have nothing to be afraid of, do you?"

Sierra actually smiled at that. "No, I guess I don't."

Dr. Cayden put her pad down and looked at her. "Okay then?"

With tears in her eyes, Sierra smiled and nodded.

"Okay then. Now, Sierra, I'm not saying that all of your problems will be solved, but I think you've taken a very big step. This is really good. This has been a very productive session."

Sierra agreed. She was exhausted, and her face was wet with tears. She was crying, really crying, in front of someone, and she'd told someone what happened, and yet the world hadn't stopped. She was still alive. Sierra smiled faintly as she realized that maybe, just maybe, for the first time since she was a little girl, she really wasn't ashamed.

Chapter 29

$\int$ ierra arrived home after the session feeling emotionally drained. She could barely remember the drive home. Her mind and body were on autopilot: one minute she was in the elevator going down to the street from Dr. Cayden's office, and the next minute she was parking her car in the condo parking lot.

She didn't even bother turning on the lights when she walked in her front door. She let the sunlight coming in through the windows lead her to her bedroom, where she kicked off her shoes and curled into a tight ball on the bed, hugging her pillow.

This feels good, she thought. She let a big, long yawn escape from her mouth and held the pillow tighter. Then she let her muscles relax and closed her eyes.

She opened her eyes seconds later and looked around her. She was in a small church that was packed to capacity. All around her, there was music. Everyone was singing. Hands were clapping. A choir stood behind the small pulpit, but they had on no robes. The voices were so powerful, they made the floor underneath her feet shake. She looked to her right; there was Mary, clapping and singing with all of her might. She looked to her left and there was John, looking just how he had when she'd last been with him in the forest.

The place was electric with excitement. Used to the dreams by now, Sierra acclimated herself to the current situation quickly. The last time she saw John, he'd spoken about a meeting at a church—and about organizing to start a campaign for getting people registered to vote. Several weeks had passed since she had that dream, and she'd thought they were over. Yet here she was, in a church, wearing a yellow dress with a white flowered print, the gold locket John gave her around her neck, singing and clapping along with everyone else.

She felt someone tug on her hand. It was John, motioning for her to have a seat. Sierra realized that the singing had stopped and everyone else was already seated. Her face grew hot; she sat down quickly and ducked her head.

Mary gave her leg a pat. "Are you all right?"

Sierra nodded reassuringly.

A man Sierra assumed was the pastor approached the pulpit. "I know that we're all excited to get started organizing and getting everyone registered. Brother John will now come up and give us direction as to how we will go about this thing. Brother John . . ."

John gave Sierra a quick peck on the cheek before maneuvering his way out of the overcrowded pew to the front of the church. As he made his way to the front, the congregation encouraged him with clapping and pats on the back.

"Thanks so much for coming tonight," John began when the pastor surrendered the pulpit to him. "And for your enthusiasm. We are really going to need that enthusiasm. We have every indication that some people may not readily receive the information and opportunity we're providing them with. They may be scared and unsure, and for very good reasons. We all know that what we're attempting to do may cause a reaction the likes of which we haven't seen before. But I think it's vital to our continued existence that we let the people of this state and the world know we won't be bullied and mistreated any longer. Not without a fight."

As John began to pull flyers out of his satchel, a woman stood up and said, "I know everyone is excited, but I want to emphasize how dangerous this is. This young man is not from around here, and he may not understand how mean and ugly this thing can get. Things have been okay for a while with us and them—and they can stay that way, as long as we don't rock the boat. Doing something like this is going to stir up resentment and anger, and I have a family to worry about."

Another woman stood up. "We all have families to worry about," she said. "But I'm looking toward my kids' futures. I don't want them to live in a world where they're not allowed to have a say in the laws being made that affect them. Resentment and anger are already here. It's already stirred up. But I'm tired of being afraid to ask for what's fair, and I want to teach my children a different type of lesson."

Amens and cheers arose, and both ladies sat down.

"No one is making anyone participate," John said. "This is simply an informational meeting. If you're interested, the details are on these flyers. And because we know how dangerous this is, we want everyone to think carefully about participating. I know I'm not from around here, but I've been here for a while. I know how things are and I know what I'm asking of all of you. Remember that I'm taking the risk with you. Change can't come unless acts of bravery facilitate it."

The pastor dismissed the service, and the congregation divided into two groups: people lining up to go to the front, and people gathering their things and heading toward the door. Mary grabbed Sierra's hand and started leading her toward the front—but before they could take a second step, a loud crash shook the room and smoke filled the air.

Panicked cries arose as the loud crashing sounds repeated themselves. Sierra coughed and hit the floor with Mary. Somehow John made it to their side right away and put his body over theirs, protecting them from the unknown danger. And then Sierra saw them: bottles strewn on the floor with fiery rags hanging out of them.

The screams were so loud that they pierced Sierra's ears. She could hear the pastor in the background, calling for everyone to stay calm and head for the door.

John grabbed Sierra's and Mary's hands and pulled them into the growing crowd that was exiting the church. The smoke filled Sierra's lungs, and she found that she could barely breathe. Her eyes were stinging, and she began to feel real terror. But then she got closer to the door and felt the cool night air hit her skin and she calmed down, reassured that soon she would be able to breathe again.

It was then that she noticed that the screams weren't only coming from the people behind and beside her—they were coming from in front of her as well, from people who had already escaped the church. As she pressed outside and her eyes cleared a bit, she could see what she couldn't before: A burning cross was there to greet the congregation as they crowded out of the church. Men dressed in white robes waited outside the church in several pickup trucks. The men jumped out of their trucks and began smashing car windows, yelling and taunting the crowd while the fires burned.

Sierra didn't know what to do. She was frozen; all she could do was stare at the horrifying scene taking place in front of her. And then she didn't have to wonder what to do, as the decision was taken from her. John was pulling her in the direction of the back of the church. Mary, on her other side, also seemed to know where they were going.

They stopped at a shed, and John immediately opened it and began to look around.

"What are you looking for?" Sierra asked.

"There's a water pump over there."

She followed the direction his finger pointed in and saw the pump a few feet away, surrounded by grass.

"I'm looking for anything we can fill with water so we can stop this fire."

Before he had even finished his sentence, Sierra and Mary were digging through the shed, helping him look.

Seconds into their search, they heard a commotion just outside, and they all paused. Then the door of the shed flew open, and the pastor and several other men from the congregation burst in.

The pastor seemed to already know what they were looking for, and he pointed them in the right direction. Everyone grabbed buckets and anything else they could find that would hold water, then rushed out of the shed toward the pump.

Sierra could smell the acrid stench from the fire in the air. It singed her nose hairs. Her eyes pooled with tears as the dark smoke from the church slowly surrounded their group, tightening its grip. Everyone was working as fast as they could: the men were pumping the water as Sierra and Mary held the containers, and then running toward the church to put the fire out. By now, others, both men and women, had made their way to the pump and were helping their efforts.

The pastor informed everyone that others had gone for help, but Sierra knew they had to help themselves—and everyone else seemed to understand that as well.

At one point, as Sierra carried a pail of water over to the church—which was now filled with dark smoke—she moved around to the front of the church. The trucks and the men in the white robes were gone; all that was left to see now was the collateral damage.

The face of the church, although now mostly free of fire, was wreathed in smoke. The entire congregation was working to finish putting the flames out, but although they were dying down, Sierra knew the church was gutted. A deep sadness filled her chest, and she knew that her tears weren't only due to the sting of the smoke in the air.

Sierra handed her container to a man who was receiving the pails at the front of the church and methodically dousing the now-small flames. As she turned away, out of the corner of her eye she noticed something bright still shining in the darkness the smoke had created. It was the burning cross.

Sierra walked over to it, careful not to get too close. Up until this point, most of the crowd's efforts had gone to putting out the fire in the church, but now that the situation was under control, a few were going back and forth to put out the fire burning the cross.

Sierra stood for a moment with her hand over eyes and mouth and took it all in—the screams, the sadness, and the anger of those around her, as well as her own grief and anger.

Looking at that cross and the burning church, she understood the bravery and commitment of the people surrounding her in a whole new way. She understood that she was a part of it. She understood that the kind of courage she was now seeing was her legacy. And then she was no longer staring but running back behind the church for more water to help.

She saw Mary at the pump and they made eye contact. An understanding glance passed between the two as they continued to work. And then the question of where John was fought through all the thoughts occupying Sierra's head. As she carried another bucket of water to the cross, she searched for him worriedly, but even in her concern she moved as fast as she could, spurred on by her new realization and conviction. She reached the cross, lifted the pail, and released the water, eager to put out the ugliness the burning cross ignited. And after she did that, she felt good. She felt free.

She was readying herself to go back for more water when someone whipped her around. Strong arms held her close. She knew those arms.

"Are you okay? I've been looking for you," John exclaimed, relief evident in his voice.

Sierra held him tight. "I've been looking for you, too."

John tightened his hold as if afraid she might disappear. "Don't do that to me again. Don't you know how much I love you?"

Sierra pulled away a little, just enough to look into his eyes. She knew those eyes.

The smoke from the now-extinguished cross began to fill the air around them. It was getting harder and harder for Sierra to see anything. She could still feel John's hands around her, even if she couldn't see him anymore, and she could hear his voice saying, "We belong together. I will never leave you. I love you . . ."

Chapter 30

$\mathcal{S}$ ierra woke up in her bed drenched in sweat and breathing heavily. She slowly allowed her body to relax—something that came much easier now than it had when she first started having these dreams. She looked down and realized that she was wearing the same clothes she'd worn to her visit with Dr. Cayden. And then it all came back to her: the anxiety and relief she'd felt during the appointment, and the total fatigue she'd felt afterward.

She stretched her arms above her head and allowed herself a good yawn. Sunlight was beginning to stream into the room through the window. Spring finally looked as though it might actually stay for a while.

She glanced over at the alarm clock and saw that it was seven in the morning. It had only been five or so when she got home on Friday, yet she had slept through the night and into the morning. She hoped she wasn't regressing, and was happy to realize that she doubted that she really was. She chalked it up to exhaustion.

Her sticky clothes continued to cling to her. She got out of bed and headed over to the bathroom, where she undressed and got in the shower. She let the hot water revive her senses as she thought about the dream she'd just woken from. Once again, she and the people in her visions, whom she now counted as friends, had found themselves in a dangerous situation—and once again, everyone had banded together and helped save one another. Everyone had been courageous.

Sierra simply couldn't forget the feeling that came over her as she doused the burning cross with water. She'd known who she was in that moment; Dorothy and Sierra were one and the same now. All the courage and faith and love that Dorothy and Mary and John had were also inside of her. *John . . .*

He'd said that he loved her. Sierra played the dream back in her head as she got out of the shower, dried off, and put on a comfortable T-shirt and some pajama pants. Mary and John were both important to her in the dream, but it was John who she was searching for at the end of the dream. It was John who said that he loved her and would love her forever.

Sierra took a seat at the chair in front of her easel by the window. When John held her and confessed his love, she felt so good. Better than she had ever imagined she could feel when someone said that to her. John was so handsome, and smart, and kind. With him, she felt like her true self. She was comfortable.

"And he's a figment of my imagination," she said aloud. "He doesn't exist."

She knew that developing such strong feelings for someone in her dreams was probably not the healthiest thing. *At this rate I'll be in therapy for another year.* This time she purposely didn't say the words out loud, lest she make the thought true.

Thinking of the therapy took her back again to yesterday's appointment. She had let her secret out. Someone else knew, and the earth continued to spin on its axis.

She looked at the blank canvas sitting on the easel before her and smiled. An idea had just come to her. She stretched her hands above her head and reached for the ceiling to get her muscles loose. Then she began to mix several different hues of blue on the palate. Once she got the perfect blue, she began to paint.

⟡

Sierra got up from her chair and realized that her legs had gone to sleep. She looked out the window and saw how high the sun was in the sky; several hours must have passed. *No wonder.* She gave her thighs a couple of punches with her fists to try and get the feeling back.

Her stomach was growling, so she headed to the kitchen. As she opened up the refrigerator, she heard her phone buzz and ring once, though the sound was muffled. She looked over into the living room and saw her purse still sitting on the couch where she'd thrown it when she got back from her appointment with Dr. Cayden. She got her phone and swiped the screen, and Steve's name came flashing up.

"Good morning. What are you doing?"

Sierra got those now-familiar butterflies in her stomach, and a huge smile began to spread across her face. "Nothing yet," she typed, "what are you doing?"

"Now that I know you're free, I want to spend the day with you."

That was Steve. He always made his feelings clear.

Sierra thought about her day yesterday and how tired and drained she was. She felt a lot better this morning, and even better after painting—but she wasn't sure if she was in the mood to socialize after dealing with something so heavy. On the other hand, one of the points of the session was to allow herself to date and trust, and she had fun with Steve. Maybe she needed a little more fun in her life.

Not "maybe," definitely! she thought. Especially considering all that she had been dealing with lately. Her mind was made up. "Ok," she texted back, "as long as we do something fun." She added a smiley face emoji, which she never used to use.

Steve responded immediately: "Deal!"

"When I said I wanted to have fun, this was not what I envisioned," Sierra said as she grabbed shoes from the rental desk at the bowling alley.

Steve grinned. "Just wait and give it a chance."

After his last text, he had called her to set up a time to get together. Once they decided on two o'clock, Steve suggested that Sierra dress comfortably and to make sure she wore socks. As per his instructions, she had dressed casually, in jeans and a comfortable turquoise top. Steve had picked her up at the appointed time, looking handsome in jeans and a gray shirt, and they headed off.

The fact that Steve suggested she wear socks should have given Sierra a hint that they might end up at a bowling alley. But it had been ages since she had bowled. The last time she could remember doing it was when she and a group of friends had gone in college. As far as she could remember, she wasn't very good at it.

The bowling alley was busy on this Saturday afternoon. Families, teenagers, and couples alike filled the chairs on every lane. Steve and Sierra headed to their designated bowling lane, and as Sierra picked out a ball that wouldn't be too heavy for her to carry but would still roll fast enough to knock down a few pins, Steve put their names into the lane computer to keep score.

Their respective missions accomplished, they both sat to change their shoes. They exchanged smiles and Steve asked, "Are you ready?"

"As ready as I'll ever be. Are you?"

"Absolutely. Ladies first!" He waved his hand toward the lane.

Sierra rolled her eyes and got her ball. "I'm not very good at this, so I hope you keep your expectations low," Sierra joked.

Steve laughed. "Don't worry about being good. Just try and have a little fun." He clapped and cheered encouragingly from his chair as Sierra walked up to the lane, making her laugh.

She stood at the line, staring the pins down, and tried to empty her mind and relax. She let her hand go back and released the ball. Steve, still cheering, came up behind her as the ball went in a straight line down the lane.

With a crash, all the pins came tumbling down and the screen above the lane screamed, "Strike!"

Sierra couldn't believe it. She jumped up and down as if she had just won a championship, shouting, "I did it, I did it!"

"Yes, you did. Are you sure you don't do this often? I think you're trying to hustle me," Steve said, laughing.

"Whatever. I promise I don't do this."

They enjoyed her victory for a while longer, and then Steve took his turn to bowl.

"All right, all right, no pressure. Just do your best and have fun," Sierra mocked, echoing his advice.

Steve shook his head and chuckled, then went up to the lane and straightened his back. When he released the ball, it flew speedily toward the center pin and knocked all the pins down . . . except for one.

He turned to Sierra, who was clapping and trying to hide a smug smile. "Good job. Good job!" she cheered.

Steve was a good sport about it; he seemed to be more interested in the good time being had than whether or not he was winning.

Sierra got up to give him a high-five, and after slapping her hand, he grabbed her up in a hug. Sierra was surprised by the move, but she allowed herself to be swept up in his embrace; she enjoyed the feel of his arms around her.

Steve didn't hold on to her for long; he set her down a second later, and as she got ready to take her next turn, he tilted his head in the direction of the snack bar. "I'll go get us some soft drinks and snacks," he said. "Don't go knocking down all the pins while I'm gone!"

They spent the rest of their time at the alley laughing and letting go. They joked, they flirted, and they had a blast. It was the first time that Sierra could remember having so much fun with another person in a long time.

CRO

Around five in the afternoon, the couple had done all the bowling they could stand for one day. Sierra had won the first game, and Steve the second and third, but it didn't matter to either one of them who won. They'd had a really good time.

As they left the bowling alley, Sierra said, "So now what?"

"Are you hungry?"

Sierra looked up and placed her finger on her chin, tapping lightly as if really giving the question some thought. "Yeah, I think I am." She wasn't sure how that was possible, since they'd eaten pizza slices and nachos throughout their time bowling, but her stomach was definitely growling.

Steve smiled. "What do you feel like eating?"

"I think I want Chinese food."

"You're ready to mix Chinese food in with all of the other things that we've eaten today?" Steve asked, laughing.

Sierra nodded and smiled. "Why not? Are you scared?"

"No, if you're willing to risk it, then I am too," he said good-naturedly. "Did you have a place in mind?"

"I sure do," she said. "I know just the place."

CRO

When they reached the restaurant, Steve didn't fail in his good manners: he opened the door for Sierra, pulled out her chair, and made her feel cared for. They ordered wontons and spring rolls for the appetizer, and beef stir-fry and kung pao chicken for the main dishes, and before and after the meal came, they continued the easy banter and conversation that had become the norm between them. They talked more about their families, their jobs, and their plans for the future, as well as Sierra's painting and Steve's coaching, while simultaneously flirting.

"I think it's great that you're painting so much," Steve said when Sierra mentioned that she'd spent that whole morning working on a new piece. "I would love to see some of your work!"

Sierra nodded. "Maybe someday I'll show you."

Steve talked about the mentoring and coaching he did at a community center near his school. "They do all sorts of activities—sports, arts and crafts, cooking. It's awesome. The kids love it, and it gives them something constructive and educational to do during the hours they aren't in school."

"Sounds like fun!"

"It really is. You should check it out."

Sierra thought back to how much fun she used to have in college with the kids she tutored and mentored. "I think I will," she said, and meant it.

They carried on at the restaurant for several more hours. Even after the wait staff had cleared all the plates and the check had been paid, Steve and Sierra sat and drank water and soft drinks, joking and laughing.

Finally, they looked up and realized that the restaurant had gotten extremely busy. The evening patrons were starting to come in. Sierra opened her purse and looked at her phone. It was nine o'clock. When she looked up again, Steve met her eyes, and he seemed to know what she was going to say before she said it.

"We should probably get going," she said regretfully.

"Are you sure? Do you want to go somewhere else?"

As much fun as Sierra had that day, she was wiped out. "No, I think I'm tired. We should probably call it a night."

ᘓᕲᔲ

When they reached Sierra's condo, Steve walked her to the front door.

"I had a really good time. Thank you," Sierra offered first.

"I'm glad," Steve said, "but did you have fun? That was the main goal today. That was my responsibility."

Sierra beamed. "That was both of our responsibility, and yes I had a lot of fun. Did you have a good time?"

Steve looked in her eyes. "If I'm with you, then that's always a good time."

Sierra glowed under the warmth of his gaze. He leaned down to kiss her and she met him halfway. Their lips met in a kiss that was both playful and brief.

All too soon, it ended, neither one seeming to want to take things too fast.

"I want to see you again," Steve whispered as he took Sierra's key and placed it in the lock.

"Okay," Sierra agreed immediately and turned the key in the lock. She pushed the door open.

"Good night, Sierra," he said, walking away still facing her, waiting for her to get inside the house before he turned away.

"Good night, Steve," Sierra replied. She flashed him a huge smile before closing her door and turning the lights on. For the rest of the night, she held on to the best feeling she'd ever had.

Chapter 31

$\int$ ierra woke up the next morning feeling well rested and happy. She rolled over and looked at the sun shining through the window. It looked as though it was going to be a beautiful Sunday morning. She turned to the alarm clock she'd set the night before for 8:00 a.m., and saw that it was 7:58; she reached over to turn it off before it rang.

She had felt so alive after the date that she'd had a hard time getting to sleep. Instead, she'd found herself working on the painting she'd started earlier in the day, and had ended up working on it for hours. When she finally headed to bed around one in the morning, she had checked her phone and noticed a text from Steve, wishing her a good night and pleasant dreams. She texted him back after climbing into bed, wishing him the same, and then set her alarm to make sure she woke up in time for church before drifting off to sleep.

Sierra couldn't remember having dreamed anything, so either she hadn't had one or she was back to having dreams that she couldn't remember. Both scenarios seemed plausible, and she wasn't sure how she felt about either one. Certainly she wouldn't miss the dreams that left her feeling terrorized.

Were they really over? Had facing one of her major fears in talking with Dr. Cayden on Friday, and then letting go and having fun yesterday, made them stop?

Maybe the lessons she needed to learn had been learned, and now the time for her dreaming was over. A sudden sadness filled Sierra at the thought. She began to grasp that she had become attached to the people in the dreams. If she had no more dreams, then there was no more Mary or John, and she loved them. Sure, she had people in her real life who reminded her of her dream-mates, but would it really be the same?

With a sigh, still turning these questions over in her mind, she pulled herself out of bed to get ready for church.

◦◦◦

Once again, Sierra hadn't let her family know that she was going to church so that she could sit apart. The service was very good; the pastor talked again about faith and applying faith in your life. Sierra found herself moved to tears for a second time.

When he gave the invitation to come forward and receive Christ, Sierra felt compelled to get up and go forward—yet she didn't. Something inside of her was still holding her back. She didn't know what it was, but she didn't feel ready.

Sunday dinner was another repeat of the prior week, with everyone pretty much getting along. She felt thankful that no one asked her about her therapy. Irene and her mom did ask about Steve and Dale; however, they seemed to take her "things are going fine" at face value, without asking for more details.

Most of the attention that evening was centered on Ron and his new job, and for that Sierra was grateful. She knew that Dr. Cayden wanted her to talk to her family about the abuse, and she would. *Just not today*, she thought. She wanted to enjoy the banter between her family members for one evening, without the spotlight turning on her—and she got her wish. She was safe. She went home that night and talked to Steve on the phone for a while before going to bed.

The rest of the week went by relatively uneventfully. Sierra showed some properties and got a seller ready to begin to stage her home for sale. After work each night, she pulled out the painting she'd begun on Saturday and painted until she got tired. She was feeling so good that she canceled her Friday appointment with Dr. Cayden. As far as she was concerned, the breakthrough had been made, verified by the absence of dreams. She felt as though now she could move on.

Wednesday came around and she found herself in the neighborhood of the community center that Steve had mentioned to her. She took a long look at the building before deciding to pull over and park. She had a little time on her hands, and it was still early afternoon, so the schools hadn't let out yet. She thought it wouldn't be very busy inside. It was a good time to check it out.

As she entered, a security guard at the door greeted her.

"Hi," Sierra said, suddenly nervous. "I'm here to see about possibly volunteering ..."

"I'll show you where to go," he immediately offered, and

walked her to the office of the director of the center. When they arrived, he knocked on the door and called, "Jim! I've got someone here to see you."

The office door opened, and a tall man with an athletic build and a friendly smile emerged. He shook Sierra's hand. "How can I help you?"

"I'm interested in learning about volunteer opportunities here," Sierra offered, and as she said the words, she felt more confident about her decision.

"Great. Let me show you around and tell you a little bit about our programs, and you can tell me about what you do, and we can see what would be a good fit," Jim said pleasantly.

They walked around the center, looking in the different rooms used for classes and tutoring, and also at the gym, where most of the athletic activities took place. Sierra told Jim about her job in real estate and about how she enjoyed painting and was pretty good at it.

"That's great!" Jim said. "We'd love to have you help with arts and crafts, and possibly tutor or mentor kids interested in art or business. You can put all your skills to use here, if you're up for it."

Sierra smiled. "I'd love to start off helping with arts and crafts," she said. "And maybe also do some mentoring, but let's hold off on that until I have a better handle on how much time I have available to help."

"Sounds perfect to me," Jim said. He walked her back to the office, where he had her fill out the volunteer paperwork, and then they nailed down one day a week for Sierra to come in and help with arts and crafts.

"How did you find out about us, by the way?" Jim asked.

"Steve is a friend of mine," she said. "He mentioned that he volunteers here, and that I might enjoy it—he told me I should check it out."

Jim smiled at the mention of Steve's name. "Steve is very active here," he said. "And well liked! That's great that he sent you our way."

The fact that Sierra had been referred by Steve seemed to confirm something to Jim; as he shook Sierra's hand again, he seemed to feel confident that this arrangement would work well.

Sierra felt the same way, though her reasons were different. As she stepped out of the building, she felt like she was taking a step in the right direction in her life. Volunteering was another new decision she felt sure she wouldn't regret.

Chapter 32

Several weeks had elapsed since Sierra's epiphany in Dr. Cayden's office, and she thought that she was making some real progress in her life. She still hadn't gone back for a follow-up appointment. She knew Dr. Cayden was bound to ask her about whether or not she had shared her story of abuse with her family when she next saw her, and she didn't want to have to admit to her that the answer was no.

She still hadn't quite found the right time to explain things to her family—at least, that's what she was telling herself. And since her homework assignment was incomplete, she didn't see any point in returning to therapy.

Besides, she still hadn't had any new dreams in the past few weeks. Between all the time she was devoting to her painting, the volunteering she was doing at the community center, and her work, she felt good about the balance in her life. She was still running her real estate business, but was allowing herself the opportunity to do things that had always been a part of her dreams and made up a portion of who she was. She felt she had herself together now.

Today, she had plans to meet Steve after work; he said he

had someplace special he wanted to take her. She had decided to explore the feelings she had for him and not let fear decide for her. She also hadn't yet completely broken it off with Dale—she still talked to him on the phone and texted him a bit—though they hadn't gone out since their last date at the movies. He kept trying to make a date with her, but each time Sierra found herself to be busy with one thing or another. She knew that she would also have to address this situation soon, but didn't feel quite ready yet.

As she drank her morning coffee, her mind wandered off, and to her surprise she found herself thinking about her last dream. She thought about her feelings for John and how they mirrored her feelings for Steve. She didn't know what to make of it.

Maybe John was there in her dreams as someone who was safe because he wasn't real, but she had real feelings for him. Maybe he was there to show her that she could let go with a man—let herself be trusting—and still be safe. She didn't know. What she did know, though, was that John and Steve had much in common. Both were strong, attentive, brave, and handsome men; both made her feel safe, desired, needed, and cherished at the same time.

Sierra sighed, and then smiled. "It's also possible that I'm overthinking this," she said aloud. Then, shaking her head, she let those thoughts go, finished her coffee, and headed out the door. She had some showings lined up for the morning.

Sierra showed a house in her mother's neighborhood to two different clients that morning, and they both seemed to take a serious interest.

After the showings, Sierra called Stefani to update her, check messages, and go over some other listings in the area. At the end of the conversation, Stefani asked her about Steve.

The old Sierra would have tactfully changed the subject, but the new Sierra was feeling much more trusting and willing to let others in. "Actually," she said, "we have a date today, and I'm really looking forward to it."

"Oh *really!*" Stefani said. "Do tell!"

"We've been hanging out for a few weeks," Sierra said. "Things are going really well. I really like him." She couldn't believe that these words were coming out of her own mouth, but she let them flow, and they felt good.

"I'm so happy and excited for you!" Stefani said. "From everything I've seen, Steve is a really good guy. I hope it works out between you two."

Sierra never knew that this kind of support could feel so good. "Thanks Stefani," she said gratefully. "I appreciate it— and I hope so too!"

When she got off the phone, she immediately started preparing for her date. Since Steve had told her he had something special planned for that night, she wanted to dress accordingly. She opted for her favorite black dress, which was simple, hugged her curves, and had a hemline that stopped just above her knee. She finished the outfit with her favorite silver statement necklace and her favorite black leather heels.

Spring had arrived and brought warmer weather along

with it for the time being. Sierra checked The Weather Channel; the forecast for that night was clear skies and temperatures in the lower sixties.

The doorbell rang as she was putting the final touches on her makeup. Instead of the anxiety that she was used to experiencing before a date, she felt only excitement.

She opened the door for Steve, and there he stood with a dozen roses in his hand and a smile on his face.

"Thank you so much," she said, accepting the flowers. "They're beautiful! Come on in."

"Hi," Steve said.

"Hi, yourself."

"You look . . . beautiful."

The way he was looking at her, she knew he meant it.

"Thank you. You look very handsome too." Sierra checked him out and approved of the dark gray dress pants and black cashmere sweater. He looked classy.

Steve smiled. "I'm glad you approve."

"So, where are we going tonight?" Sierra inquired.

Steve shook his head. "It's a surprise, remember?"

"Okay, okay," Sierra said, chuckling. "I'll be ready in just a couple of minutes. Make yourself comfortable."

Sierra knew Steve would look around the living room and kitchen areas while she was gone, making note of the parts of her personality that showed through in her décor. She had taken care to place her paintings and supplies in the guest room. She didn't want her living room to look cluttered, but more than that, she was still a little shy about anyone seeing her work.

Within a couple of minutes, Sierra was walking back into

the living room with her purse and lightweight jacket, ready to go. Steve helped her put her jacket on, and they were off.

Steve's car was waiting at the curb, and he opened Sierra's door and got her settled before going to the driver's side and sliding in behind the wheel. He gave her a smile and a quick look of approval again before taking off.

Steve asked about Sierra's week and Sierra talked about a few showings and said that she'd finished the last painting she'd been working on and had started a new one. Steve wanted her to describe it, but Sierra didn't really think she could do it justice. She also knew that since he had no knowledge of the dreams she had been having, or her abuse in the past, it would be even harder for him to understand the significance the painting held for her.

"It's just hard to put into words," she tried to explain.

Steve nodded in understanding. "Maybe you don't have to. I would love to see it."

Sierra had originally been flattered when Steve and even Dale had expressed interest in seeing her paintings. But now, after thinking about it, she was reluctant. She hadn't shown anyone her paintings since college, and then only her instructor and fellow students in the class had seen her canvases. Sharing her work had been part of the experience in the class. She wasn't sure how she would feel having someone whose opinion she cared about look at her work.

I guess I'll find out, she thought. "If you want to, you can have a look when I'm sure I'm really done with it."

"I would like that a lot," Steve said.

The rest of the ride was Steve talking about his basketball team and how they were going to the championship. He invited Sierra to come and support them. Sierra told him that she would try.

They made it to their destination quickly. They were still downtown and now at the Milwaukee River, where the boats docked for riverboat rides.

"Is this what we're doing?" Sierra asked, her face lighting up. "A riverboat ride?"

"You guessed it!" Steve said.

Sierra was excited. Even though she'd lived in Milwaukee most of her life, she hadn't taken a riverboat ride since she was a child. That had been a family outing, and was a happy memory.

Steve parked the car and got out to open Sierra's door. She noticed a little bounce in his step as he led her forward to the well-lit boat docked before them, his hand on the small of her back.

The boat was neither empty nor overly full. Most people were standing along the deck near the balcony, admiring the view of the Milwaukee Harbor and the surrounding restaurants. Soft music was playing in the background. Steve led Sierra to a less heavily populated area so they could enjoy the view together and have some level of privacy.

"Well, what do you think so far?" he asked.

"I think it's beautiful," Sierra said, giving his hand a squeeze. "Thank you so much for bringing me here."

"You're welcome," Steve responded, looking very pleased.

They stood quietly talking for another ten minutes, and

then they heard the loud whistle of the big vessel as it cast off. After the boat began to move, the chill from the river had Sierra wrapping her arms around her body. Steve, noticing, stood behind her and enfolded her in his embrace, pulling her close to his chest. She leaned into him, enjoying the warmth that took away the cold, and let her head rest on his chest.

A short while later, a speaker above them crackled to life, and an announcement was made inviting everyone still on the deck to come in, as dinner service was about to start.

Upon entering the interior of the boat where dinner was to take place, Sierra admired the ambiance of the room. Lit candles on every table shed a romantic glow, adding to the soft lighting already present. On the walls were nautical pictures and souvenirs, as well as photos of well-known sights from around the downtown Milwaukee area.

The tables were covered with pale cream tablecloths and set with flower bouquet centerpieces. The hostess led Sierra and Steve to a table toward the center of the room, and Steve pulled out Sierra's chair for her before taking his own seat. Seconds later, the server came with menus and water.

"I'll be back in a few moments for your drink order," he said before heading over to another table.

Sierra took the opportunity to turn to Steve and express her gratitude again. "This is all very nice. Thank you."

He took her hand from where it was sitting on top of her menu. "I'm just really glad you like it, and I hope you're having a good time."

"Of course I am."

"Good," he said, caressing her fingers.

Sierra made no effort to pull away. She enjoyed the feel of her hand in his.

When the waiter returned, they put in their drink and dinner orders. When the waiter walked away, Steve sat up straighter in his chair, as if preparing himself for something.

"So . . ." he began.

"So . . ." Sierra repeated with a smile.

"So, we've been going out for a few weeks now."

Sierra nodded and smiled again, not sure where he was going with this. "Yes, we have."

"And I've enjoyed every minute of it."

Sierra smiled again, shyly this time. "Me too."

"Good. Sierra, I want you to know that I really like you."

Sierra's heart fluttered a little. "I like you too."

"Thank you," Steve acknowledged with a grin before continuing. "No, Sierra, I mean I really like you. As in, I can see us being together for as far into the future as I can imagine."

"Okay . . ." Sierra returned, a little confused now.

"What I'm saying is that I want us to be exclusive. I don't want to date anyone but you, and I want to be the only one you're dating."

The confusion cleared. "Oh . . . I see," Sierra said. She took a moment to think about it. Her feelings for Steve were very strong—so much stronger than anything she was feeling for Dale. Only her fear had been holding her back from allowing herself to really commit to her feelings for Steve, and she had no problem with that now. If he could put his feelings out there, then so could she. She was ready.

"Okay," she said.

Steve furrowed his eyebrows. "Okay . . ."

"Okay, let's make this exclusive," she said with a smile.

Steve grinned and reached across the table, gently guiding her toward him so he could kiss her waiting lips. The kiss was gentle and sweet, and it was Sierra who extended the kiss when Steve would have pulled away. That brought a smile to Steve's lips, which Sierra could feel under her own, which she enjoyed almost as much as the kiss itself.

They broke apart only when the waiter returned with their drinks and a basket of rolls.

After dinner service was over, people began to move to the deck again to watch the scenery around them. Sierra and Steve went out on the deck as well. The private corner they'd found in the beginning was still available and they took that spot. From there, they gazed at the shoreline of Lake Michigan before the boat turned and headed back to its home.

"This has been the best night," Sierra commented.

"For me too," Steve agreed before turning her around and kissing her again.

As they stood there on the deck in embrace, Sierra had never been happier. She had a sneaking suspicion that she might be falling in love.

Chapter 33

The day after her cruise with Steve, Sierra called Dale and broke off whatever was left of a romantic relationship with him. She felt nervous putting all her eggs in one basket, but she felt more like her Dorothy self taking risks and following her heart, even if that meant doing something scary, and that felt good.

The phone conversation itself was pleasant enough. Dale took the news well—almost too well for Sierra's liking.

"I'm glad you're taking this so well," she said. She attempted to keep her tone good-natured, but a little bit of edge crept in. Even though she knew being offended by someone taking a letdown so well wasn't logical, she couldn't help but feel a little insulted.

Dale laughed. "Sierra, I knew something was going on. Every time you were with me, you were preoccupied. I like you and I have a lot of fun with you, but just like you, I want someone who is totally into me and returns the feelings that I have for her."

That made sense. Sierra had to laugh at herself for her own reaction. She wanted Dale to have a real relationship too. He was a good guy.

They joked around for a few more minutes after that and then ended the phone call amicably. After hanging up, Sierra sat on her couch with a feeling of accomplishment. She turned on the television, lay down on her side, and turned the channels until she found a good movie. It was a comedy that she'd seen many times before, but she never grew tired of it. She could watch it a hundred times and it would still make her laugh.

Toward the end of the movie, she found herself getting sleepy. She burrowed her body deeper into the couch and grabbed a couple of decorative pillows to place behind her head. When the credits began to roll, she slowly closed her eyes with a smile on her face, still laughing at the movie.

When Sierra opened her eyes, she instantly knew that she was dreaming. She was lying down in a bed in a dark room with only a little light coming through the crack in the door she was facing. She could hear breathing next to her. She turned and found that she was facing Diana, who was sound asleep.

Sierra began to panic. She looked down at her hands and realized that they were little hands; she looked at her body and discovered that she was wearing the nightgown she'd worn when she was little. She was her little girl self.

As she took in the room and situation, more dread set in. Many years had passed since she'd thought about this night, and now she was living it again.

Then a squeaky noise had Sierra turning back toward the door, and the light in the doorway revealed Wayne, standing in the hallway. He stood there for a second, looking at Sierra and smiling that weird odd smile that he reserved for her, before creeping up to the bed and tugging on Sierra's arm, trying to get her to come with him.

But she wouldn't. Sierra didn't want to go. She knew what would happen.

She didn't want any more trips to the attic. She wouldn't go tonight. She hugged Diana and held on for dear life.

Wayne began to slowly try and untangle her fingers from Diana's arm, but Sierra refused to let go. She held on tighter.

Wayne's face darkened. "Let her go," he hissed in a threatening tone.

Sierra continued to hold on, but Wayne began to win—Sierra could feel her body easing toward the edge of the bed. She looked up, and with tears in her eyes, as she had done so many times, she asked the Lord for help.

Suddenly, a light was shining above her head. The movement toward the edge of the bed stopped. She felt a hand on her hand, giving her strength. She felt another hand on her body, keeping it still. Diana began to stir.

Sierra felt Wayne let go. She saw him looking above her head, awestruck and trembling. He slowly backed up. Keeping his eyes on the area above Sierra's head, he opened the door and rushed out without a word.

Diana settled back into sleep. The hand that was on Sierra's hand eased its hold, and Sierra gazed up and saw what appeared to be two angels. They smiled down at her, giving her comfort. Somehow, Sierra knew their faces.

She reached out to touch them, and as she did, she closed her eyes. When she opened them again, she was reaching into the air above her couch in her condo. She was awake.

Sierra sat up slowly into a sitting position and ran her fingers through her hair as she tried to make sense of what had just happened.

She had known where she was as soon as she'd opened her eyes in the dream. This was no dream about Dorothy. This was a dream about Sierra. Except this time it wasn't just a dream—that night had really happened. It was the last time Sierra could remember Wayne trying to molest her.

The dream, however, was different from how she had always remembered that night. Was it possible that angels really had been there helping her the whole time, giving her strength? Sierra was full of so many emotions right now that she couldn't quite make sense of anything. She had always assumed that she made Wayne stop on the merit of her own strength. That he had gotten tired of pulling her and hadn't wanted to wake his cousin.

For so many years, Sierra thought that she had continually asked God for help and He had abandoned her. After that night, she had been angry with God, and had isolated herself from family and friends. She figured no one had helped her then, and since she, alone, was the one who had gotten Wayne to stop, she could only rely on herself. And she had, for all of these years.

Sierra put her head in her hands, pondering the possibility that she had never been alone after all—that some of the isolation, fear, and anger she felt might have been self-inflicted. She shook her head, still not fully knowing what to think. If God hadn't abandoned her, maybe *she* had abandoned *Him*.

If her dream was true, where did she go from here?

Chapter 34

*T*he weather was milder that Sunday, and so was Sierra's disposition. She had made plans with her family to have Sunday dinner at her mom's house, as usual, but with one caveat: she had requested that no children be present, because she had something personal to discuss with her mom, Irene, and Ron.

To her surprise, no one had made a fuss; Jason had agreed to keep the kids that Sunday and do some fun activities with them, and the rest of her family had seemed eager to see what the announcement was, as sharing anything personal was not in Sierra's nature. Sierra's mom was hoping that this would perhaps be an announcement of a pending engagement, but Irene tempered her mom's enthusiasm by reminding her that it would be a little early for that, regardless of who Sierra was currently dating.

Sierra made her way to church early, guaranteeing herself a seat in the sanctuary. She again decided against telling her family that she was coming to service; she was making great strides in her relationship with God, and she could take in information better when she felt she wasn't being watched.

She knew that her family was eager for her to become a member of the church, and she was moving in that direction, but it would have to happen on her own timeline.

Sierra settled into the section she'd occupied on her last visit. The view was perfect: not too close and not too far.

The service progressed in a normal fashion. First came music and worship, followed by offering and the announcements. Finally, the pastor, dressed in a simple black suit with a crisp white shirt, took the pulpit.

He began the sermon by having the congregation once again stand and pray. Then he explained that today he would be talking about faith's opposition—fear. He asked the congregation to turn to II Timothy 1:7.

"The scripture reads thusly," Pastor Miller said. "'For God hath not given us the spirit of fear: but of power, and of love, and of a sound mind.' Today, we address fear and how if we allow it to run our lives, it can destroy not only our hopes and our dreams but even the success in the lives we are currently living. We have talked about faith and the importance of living our lives every day by faith, but we must also acknowledge that faith cannot work together with fear. We all make a decision to live in one or the other. And it is a decision that we wake up and make every single day." He looked out at the congregation, his gaze searching. "God has made promises to you about how life will be if you keep his commandments and stand on his word. He teaches us to trust in Him and His word and to not trust in what we see. He promises that if we can do that, then everything will work out for our good. Fear, on the other hand, does something entirely different. Fear paralyzes you from taking any action. Fear takes control of your life and causes you to live a life that's less than. Fear causes you sleepless nights, poor health, and eventually death. The choice is simple. Choose life. Choose faith."

Pastor Miller went on to talk about the importance of prayer and asking for help from the Lord, quoting Psalm 23:4 and Psalm 91, among other scriptures.

As Sierra sat and listened, she felt moved once again by his words and how he seemed to be ministering directly to her. By the end of the sermon, she could feel tears welling up in her eyes. She opened her purse and took out some tissues that she now kept stored there. Over the past few months, she'd gone from someone who never showed emotion to someone who regularly let her emotions go. She felt liberty in being that kind of person.

Soon, the pastor was once again figuratively "opening the doors of the church" and calling people forward who wanted to receive Christ as their personal savior or join the church. Sierra felt a pressing in her spirit that was propelling her to get up and walk to the front of the church. She'd felt it the last time she was there but hadn't followed the feeling; she hadn't wanted to get up and have to walk in front of everybody, including members of her family.

It's not that I'm ashamed, she thought. *It's just that I'm ... I'm ...*

And then she knew: the word she was looking for was "afraid." As she realized that fear was what was holding her back, she felt her body stand as if of its own volition. Immediately the people around her offered their encouragement, clapping and cheering her on. Sierra grabbed her purse and headed to the front of the church. The cheering got louder and louder as she got closer and closer to the pulpit.

Two other people from the congregation—a young mother carrying her baby and an older gentleman—had also accepted Pastor Miller's invitation and were already standing in the front of the church ahead of Sierra. As she approached them, she felt braver and braver. She wasn't alone. Everyone was smiling and encouraging her. She felt good. She was almost there.

As she walked the last five feet, she felt someone on her left take her hand. She turned her head and found her mother standing next to her. She looked at her and smiled, and the tears in her mother's eyes mirrored the tears in her own eyes.

She then felt someone take her right hand. She knew before looking that it would be Irene, and it was.

Sierra was two feet away from the front of the church now, and she had her sister on one side and her mom on the other, holding tightly to her hand.

And then there she was, at the front of the church—and just as her mom and sister let go of her hand to stand behind her in support, she felt a third hand on her back. It was Ron, visibly trying to hold back tears. All three of them encompassed Sierra in a hug of support, even as she could still hear the rest of the congregation applauding in the background. They embraced Sierra so tight she had trouble breathing, but she didn't mind.

"Will the three brave people who have come to the front please lift their hands to God?" Pastor Miller boomed from the pulpit.

The arms that held her so tightly let go, and Pearl, Irene,

and Ron stood behind Sierra while she told the Lord that she believed in Him and was this day giving her life to Him.

I'm home, Sierra thought as she made her promise. Today was a day of reunion—with her family and with her faith. She was healing and all the broken pieces in her life were coming together.

Chapter 35

*A*fter church, Sierra, Pearl, Irene, and Ron headed back to Pearl's house, as was the original plan. When they arrived, Sierra found that her mom already had a turkey prepared, along with some dressing and greens, so all she had to do was heat the food up. *That's my mom,* she thought appreciatively. *Always prepared.*

Pearl put the food on the stovetop and in the oven to warm as soon as they walked into the house, and then she and Ron left Sierra and Irene to their own devices while they went into their respective bedrooms to change clothes. The sisters settled in on the couch in the living room to wait.

The whole house already smelled like apple pie, which was what their mom had made for dessert. The smells reminded Sierra of her dream at Miss Patty's, which reminded her of her mom's house, and she laughed at the confusing thought.

As Irene grabbed the remote and began to search for something to watch, she noticed Sierra's chuckle. "What's so funny?"

Sierra only shook her head and said nothing.

Irene smiled and shrugged, and they sat there in comfortable silence.

Soon, Ron and Pearl emerged from their rooms. Pearl immediately went to the kitchen to tend to the food, while Ron seated himself on the lounge chair next to the couch.

"Can you turn it to the game?" he asked, gesturing toward the TV.

Irene and Sierra looked at each other and smiled, and Irene switched to the sports channel. They didn't mind at all.

The whole scene reminded Sierra of the times they would all gather in the living room with popcorn and soda when her dad was alive. Back then, he had always taken his seat in "his chair" to watch the game. Now Ron was the one in the chair.

All three watched the game in silence for a few minutes. The Bucks weren't playing, but two good teams known for their superstars were. It would be a good game.

Pearl entered the living room and sat down with a winded sigh. "Dinner will be ready in about ten minutes or so. I put some rolls in the oven and am heating up the food."

They all turned to her with smiles of acknowledgment.

"It smells really good, Mom," Ron said.

Their relationship had become more and more amicable since Ron was working, and Ron had already made a six-month plan to move out and into his own apartment. Sierra was proud of him; it seemed like he was finally growing up.

"Sierra, I was so happy to see you join the church today, it really blessed me," Pearl said, threatening tears once again.

"I'm happy too, Mom," Sierra said.

They all then looked at Sierra expectantly. It had been her idea to have dinner with just them, after all. Sierra realized that now was as good a time as any. She picked up the remote where it lay beside Irene and turned the television off. She took one more breath for bravery, then plunged in.

"Look, you guys, I wanted just you here today to tell you about something that happened to me a long time ago. It may be part of the reason that I've been having those bizarre dreams." She shrugged. "Anyway, you all probably know by now that I've been seeing someone, a therapist. I imagine if I haven't personally told you that certainly you've been discussing it amongst yourselves."

Ron, Irene, and Pearl looked at each other knowingly and didn't deny it.

"Well, we had what was kind of a breakthrough a couple of weeks ago, and she thought it would be a good idea if I discussed what happened to me with you guys."

They all continued to look at Sierra with concern, but also encouragement, in their eyes.

"Whatever it is, we're listening, baby," Pearl said, and Ron and Irene nodded in agreement.

Sierra took a deep breath, knowing she needed to get right to the point. It would be easier that way, like ripping off a Band-Aid. "Well," she said matter-of-factly, "when I was younger, I was molested."

Everyone's faces registered shock and alarm.

"By who?" Irene was the first to speak.

"It was Diana's cousin that used to live with them. You remember, Mom. She used to be my best friend."

Sierra's mom nodded in remembrance, a pained look on

her face. "When you two were friends, you couldn't have been more than five or six years old," she recollected.

Sierra nodded. "You're right, I was no older than that."

Tears fell steadily down Pearl's face. She grabbed Sierra's hands. "Why didn't you tell me? Don't you know I would have moved heaven and earth to protect you? I still would."

Sierra put her hands over her mother's, trying to comfort her. "I know that you would have. I didn't know why I never said anything, but I've come to realize lately that it was because I was ashamed, and I thought that somehow it was my fault. I mean, I kept going over there. I never told you."

Simultaneously, they all jumped to deny that it could have possibly been her fault. Once again, she was moved by their support and felt her own tears forming.

"I know that now. I guess I was just scared and ashamed. Once it happened the first time and I didn't say anything, the shame built up so much inside I thought no one would believe that I didn't want him to do it—because I didn't tell after the first time. I mean, it didn't help that he drilled that very fact into me. He made me believe that it was my fault."

"But you know now, I mean you really know now, that it wasn't your fault, right?" Irene said.

"Yes, I know that now."

"Listen, if you're okay with it, I would like to know when this all started and how long it went on," Pearl said slowly, obviously not wanting to hurt Sierra any further but needing to know.

"Yeah, that's okay," Sierra said. "That's why I asked to have this dinner with you guys, so we could talk about it and so it will no longer be my secret, eating away at me. It seems the more I talk about it, the less power it has over me."

And so Sierra started from the beginning, revealing the first time to the last. She shared that it went on for about a year. She paused at the parts that were graphic, not sure how much she wanted to reveal in front of Ron, or any of them, for that matter. But she was as honest as she could be. She answered their questions as they came, and they all sat and talked and cried together.

Pearl kept apologizing and saying that she felt as though it was all her fault. She wanted to try and do something to make it up to her. She assured Sierra that she would look into the matter. "I want to see that boy prosecuted to the full extent of the law," she said.

Sierra shook her head. "I don't need you to do that, Mama," she said. "I'm over it now—or at least, I'm in the process of being over it. All I want to do is to try and live my best life right now. I don't want to have to go to court and relive everything for strangers. I just want to be free. And besides, I'm not sure about the statute of limitations on something like that."

Pearl nodded as if she understood, but Sierra knew by the look in her eyes that she wasn't ready to let it go. "I still think it's worth looking into," she said.

Suddenly, Sierra felt Irene's whole body weight as she grabbed Sierra in a fierce hug. "I thought I was your protector," she said. "I tried to shield you from everything. I'm so sorry I failed you."

Sierra rubbed Irene's back. "You didn't fail me. You have been a really good big sister and protector, even when I didn't want you to be. It's hard to help when someone doesn't ask for it."

"Even still . . . I'm sorry." Irene was sobbing now.

And then Ron joined in. "I'm sorry too. I really am."

Sierra smiled, not really sure what Ron was apologizing for, as he was only a baby when it happened.

With tears in his eyes, he clarified, "I'm sorry that this happened to you."

Sierra took all of their love and support and hugged it into herself. She knew now that this was family. This was what it was all about.

After about another ten minutes of sobbing, hugging each other, and cursing Wayne, a loud growl from Sierra's stomach broke up the tears.

They all actually looked at each other and laughed.

Sierra was ready to let this go. She was ready to eat. She had never felt closer to her family than she did at this moment. She was the first to rise to her feet and head for the kitchen.

Everyone else seemed reluctant to go and eat after such a revelation, but they followed Sierra without protest.

Pearl shook her head and headed straight for the oven as she entered the kitchen. "Those rolls are probably burnt by now, don't you think?" she said, laughing. She opened the oven door and pulled out a tray of very well-done rolls as her children all grabbed a seat around the kitchen table.

The kitchen was warm and cozy, and the love in the room reverberated off the walls and through the air as the family of four ate their dinner.

Yes, Sierra thought. *This is what matters.*

Chapter 36

Sierra felt as if she were floating. A soft melody was playing all around her. Her head was enveloped by the softest cushion she'd ever felt. The smell in the air was familiar. It smelled of home cooking and friends. It was dark, but she was pretty sure that her eyes were closed. She slowly opened her eyes and looked around. The pictures, the sounds, the smells—she remembered this place. It was Miss Patty's house. Sierra was lying on the couch, and she could see both Miss Patty and Mary sitting at the kitchen table and having a cup of coffee. As she raised herself into a sitting position, both women got up and approached the couch.

"How are you feeling?" Miss Patty asked, smiling at Sierra.

Sierra checked herself, confused. Had she sustained some type of injury at the church? She recalled the flames, the smoke, the sounds of glass breaking. She lifted her hands to her face and checked for any areas of pain in her arms and legs. From what she could feel, she thought she was fine. "I'm okay," she said.

Mary and Miss Patty nodded in unison and smiled knowing smiles at one another.

Sierra was confused. What was going on? Why was she

here? Had something else happened? Was John hurt? What was happening?

Before Sierra was able to voice any of her concerns, Miss Patty shook her head and said, "No, child."

Sierra was now even more confused, since she hadn't actually spoken what she was thinking. She felt a frown etch across her face, and Mary took a finger and smoothed out the wrinkle that presented itself. As Mary touched her forehead, Sierra felt an ease flow from that digit through her, calming her spirit. She still wanted to know what was going on, though.

"We're coming to you because this will be the end of your seeing us for a while, but we want you to know that even if you can't see us, we will always be with you," Mary said.

Sierra shook her head. "I don't understand. What is this? What do you mean?"

The two women sat down on either side of Sierra and held each of her hands in their own.

"We needed to teach you—we needed to show you who you are," Miss Patty said, patting Sierra's hand. "We needed to show you your strength, because you had forgotten. We needed to show you your faith, because you couldn't see it. We needed to show you these things, so we showed you who you are in your dreams."

"You were never weak," Mary went on, smiling. "You were always strong. You were always capable of amazing things, and you accomplished many of them before now, but we needed to show you how much more infinitely powerful you would be if you let fear go. We needed to help you see who you could be if you allowed yourself to flow in the spirit that already lives inside of you, to trust that."

Tears flowed down Sierra's cheeks as she began to understand. The two women rested their heads on her shoulders,
and her body shook as she wept.

Miss Patty wiped the tears from Sierra's face. "Close your
eyes so that you can see," she whispered.

Sierra slowly closed her eyes, and darkness was all around
her. And then she saw it. She was back in Diana's room on
the night when Wayne had tried to take her out of the bed.
She was a child. The fear and terror from that night became
real again. But this time, she could still feel Mary and Miss
Patty holding her hands. She held on to that warmth, taking
security from it.

As Wayne entered the room, the light from the open
door pierced Sierra's eyes, just as it had before. He rounded
the bed and pulled the covers a little way off of Sierra's body,
beckoning her to come along quietly while he put his finger
to his lips as a sign to remain quiet. Diana stirred in her
sleep, but didn't wake up.

Sierra felt scared, and she didn't want to get up. She held
on to her friend. Wayne began to tug harder. Sierra held on
tighter. She was crying now and praying in her head, asking
God to help her.

Sierra's adult self recalled that it was around this time
that Wayne started to get frustrated and make angry gestures
because he couldn't get her out of the bed. She had always
thought that her resistance to him that night had been born
of her own strength. She'd thought that she was alone. That
God had abandoned her. She remembered that feeling. Both
the child and the adult Sierra wept harder.

Suddenly, a light shone from above Sierra's head. She

could see Miss Patty and Mary in the room with her. Translucent and dressed in robes, they both had an ethereal glow. They were at once floating above her and lying right next to her on the bed.

Mary held her hand against Sierra's right hand, which was holding on to Diana. Sierra could feel the strength radiating through that connection. Meanwhile, Miss Patty grabbed Wayne's hand—the hand that was trying so desperately to pull Sierra out of bed—and Sierra could see that she was weakening his hold. He looked up, frightened, and seemed to see Miss Patty there. The sight frightened him enough to want to let go.

Sierra's eyes flew open. She was back on the couch in Miss Patty's living room. Miss Patty and Mary were still holding her hand.

"It was you two. You were there?"

They nodded in unison.

"We are always there," Mary said. "God never abandoned you."

Sierra let their hands go. She couldn't accept that. Too many bad things had happened. Why had they done nothing the other times this happened? Why had they continued to allow bad things to happen to her at other times in her life? She felt hurt and confused.

"Even when bad things have happened in your life, we have still always been there, helping," Miss Patty said. "That's why we wanted you to see this, so that you could understand when you ask for help, you have it."

"And even when you don't ask for help, help is always there," Mary said. "It might not necessarily come directly from us. It might come from the people you have around you. But you are never alone."

"You ask us where were we when the bad things happened," Miss Patty said. "The answer is, we were with you, helping to prevent those bad things from becoming worse. You have no idea the trouble we block and move away from you every day."

"You might not always feel us," Mary said. "You might not always understand. But we are always with you. You are never alone."

Sierra shook her head in confusion once again, but even as she did, she sensed some clarity in her spirit.

Mary and Miss Patty looked at her with warmth. Sierra looked down, and she saw that once again, her hands were in theirs. She hadn't realized they had rejoined their hands.

And then it was happening again—the room was getting darker, and Sierra was floating.

This time, when she opened her eyes, she was in her own bedroom. Her pillow was wet with her tears. She lay there for a long time, her heart clear with understanding, her mind murky with confusion.

Chapter 37

*A*s Sierra locked her car and walked the short way to
Dr. Cayden's office, she breathed in a long, glorious
breath of summer air. Milwaukee in June didn't always mean
sunshine and warm breezes, but today that was exactly what
the weather was offering her. She paused just outside of the
doctor's building and noticed the foliage on the trees coming
alive in healthy green hues. The manicured patch of grass
surrounding the tree had also succumbed to the jade tone
that pronounced that summer was upon the city.

The sidewalk, once enveloped in muddy snow, now
gleamed in readiness for the heavy traffic of feet that the
summer festivals downtown and on the lakefront would at-
tract. Sierra smiled as she recognized the signs of a new beginning for the earth. The sun kissed her face, and she knew
that this was her new beginning as well.

She hadn't been back to see Dr. Cayden since having the
epiphany about her molestation. A little over a month had
passed since then. It had taken Sierra a while to have the talk
with her family, but now she would finally be able to report
progress.

Sierra entered the building and stepped on the elevator, feeling good about her place in the world and how well the encounter with her family had gone. Her revelation and its aftermath had gone better than anything she could have asked for. The support she'd received from her family was amazing.

Sierra stepped off the elevator and said hi to Gail, who smiled and waved her to a seat.

"Dr. Cayden will be right with you," she said cheerily.

Sierra remembered how she'd thought no way did this woman have any troubles and smirked to herself now, realizing how very wrong she could be. Just a few months ago, strangers would have envied her and thought that she had it all together, too. The truth was that you just never know.

The doctor's door opened, and Dr. Cayden welcomed Sierra with a smile. "Come on in, Sierra," she said, waving her over.

Today, Dr. Cayden was wearing a black pencil skirt and a white cotton top. Her hair was in its usual knot. Some things were changing while others stayed the same. *That's life.*

Sierra walked to the couch and took a seat without being asked.

Dr. Cayden closed the door and settled into her own chair before asking, "So, how have you been?"

Sierra exhaled and then breathed in again, not with anxiety but with the joy of embracing the precious minutes of life. "I've been really good."

Dr. Cayden nodded. "I can see that. You have a glow about you. Tell me more."

"I feel, for the first time in a long time, like I'm free. Not only free—I feel I know myself in a way that I didn't before. I feel I know my family in a way that I didn't before, and it all feels very good."

"So, I take it you've spoken to your family about the abuse."

"Yes, I did."

"And what was their reaction?"

"They were sad because they didn't know and I didn't tell them. They were hurt because they weren't there to help. But mostly they were sad because it happened to me."

Dr. Cayden nodded again. "And do you feel that they support you?"

Sierra smiled. "I know that they do. I now know that no matter what, they always do. My mom even wanted to try and press charges, but the statute of limitations was already up. And then she started looking for him anyway, and it turns out he died about five years ago. Apparently he had a heart attack."

Dr. Cayden's eyebrow lifted slightly. "How did it make you feel when you learned that he had died?"

"I honestly didn't feel too much of anything. I mean, I really hope that he didn't hurt anyone else, but he's dead now. I think anger would be a wasted emotion. It's over. I survived, so I win."

"And having your family's support, how does that make you feel?"

"It makes me feel wonderful. It makes me feel loved. It makes me feel cared for."

Dr. Cayden smiled. "I'm glad to hear that."

Sierra smiled back. "Me too."

238 | Denese Shelton

"And the dreams, what about the dreams? Have you had any more dreams lately?"

Sierra's serenity faded just a little, as she was still somewhat shaken from the last dream. She'd come to better terms with it in the last several days, but she still had so many questions. She wondered if Mary and Miss Patty were her "assigned angels." Even having heard the explanations they offered, she wondered why, if they were really angels, they hadn't protected her from everything that had hurt her. She also wondered if John was an angel. Needless to say, she hadn't quite worked everything out in her mind yet and didn't know if she ever would. But she wasn't sure she needed to. She just knew that she was happy in this moment and that was how she wanted to take life going forward: moment to moment.

"Well, I've had dreams," she finally said, "but I feel that they don't overwhelm me now. They just make me think."

"Can you tell me about these last dreams you've had?"

Sierra had thought that today would be a day of good reflections and revelations; she hadn't thought that she would have to delve into her bizarre subconscious again. But now she recognized that she needed to. Doing otherwise would just be an affirmation that she was a slave to her fear.

So, once again, she launched into her dream world, starting with the fire at the church and ending with the last dream, where Mary and Miss Patty revealed themselves as angels. Just as before, Dr. Cayden held on to her poker face, never divulging any change in emotion.

"Well," she said when Sierra was done, "I would say that

these dreams, although different in some ways, still suggest the themes that were in most of the other dreams."

"Yeah, and what themes are those?"

"They all say that you're not alone, that you have support all around you. They also communicate the idea that you're strong, and that you're necessary. Would you agree with that?"

Sierra nodded. "Yes, I was thinking the same thing."

"You told me before that you believe in God."

"Yes, I do," Sierra said emphatically.

"Perhaps the angels and that part of the dream are a reflection of your spiritual beliefs."

"Perhaps." Sierra wasn't convinced.

"You know, Sierra, when you first came in here, you were overloaded with secrets and guilt. You weren't able to sleep at night, or you would sleep too much, which I think was a sign that you were depressed. You started to have these dreams that actually forced you to take a long, hard look at yourself and to deal with the issues that you hid deep inside."

Everything Dr. Cayden was saying was true. Sierra had been quite a mess when she first came in.

"If nothing else, I would say that we can thank the dreams for forcing your hand, for waking you up, right?"

Sierra smiled. "Yeah, I'm awake now—every day I'm awake."

"Good," Dr. Cayden said. "I think we all should be."

Chapter 38

Steam floated from the top of the large pot resting on low temperature on her mother's stove. The steam danced harmoniously with the smell of the seafood gumbo, making Sierra's stomach growl. She was ready for some good eating.

She was sitting at the kitchen table, listening with amusement as her mom and sister interrogated Steve again. He'd met the entire family a couple of weeks before—on a Sunday similar to this one. At his insistence, he had gone to church with her. Steve actually belonged to a different church but wanted to experience her church service that Sunday. He and Sierra sat separately from her family on that day, giving him a reprieve until the actual meeting, scheduled to take place at her mom's house after the service. In retrospect, though, Sierra realized that the reprieve had been more for her than for him. Steve had no problem answering any question that was posed.

And boy, did her family probe. As soon as Sierra and Steve walked through the door that first Sunday, Jason and Ron had stood there with their arms folded and frowns on their faces, looking like members of the mafia.

Steve hadn't reacted. He simply answered their questions,

calmly and politely, and then let himself be ushered to sit on the couch while Irene's kids used him as a human trampoline. After a while, he had been summoned into the kitchen, where the interrogation had continued. All day he had smiled and answered—or refrained from answering, when the questions became too personal—without losing his cool. All in all, Sierra had been impressed. Based on that performance, she would have continued their relationship even if her family hadn't approved. Happily, though, they did.

Now Steve was back for a second round. Her mom and Irene had let up for the moment, and now he was going back and forth with Ron over who the best basketball player of all time was. Ron gave the title to Lebron James, while Steve insisted it belonged to Michael Jordan.

She was glad that her family actually liked and accepted Steve. She felt better about that than she cared to admit. Everyone she loved was in the same room, talking and sharing, spooning heaps of delicious gumbo into their bowls over rice.

Right in the middle of bringing a spoonful of tasty shrimp and roux into her mouth, Sierra realized that when she thought about everyone she loved, she was looking at Steve.

She loved Steve. Just for a moment, the thought paralyzed her with fear. Then Steve turned to her and smiled, giving her the look he always had when he looked at her: like she was the woman of his dreams. With that, Sierra relaxed. She knew that look, and she knew he loved her too, because he had already said so.

Sierra looked back at him with an expression that matched his. He was, after all, the man of her dreams.

Chapter 39

S ierra looked around the art exhibit displaying all she'd done in the last year. She couldn't believe that she'd gotten the opportunity to do something like this. This was her show, with her paintings. All of her family was here. Stefani, Steve, and Sierra's students from the community center were all here too.

Several months before, she'd been at the center working with the children when an owner of a gallery downtown had come in to talk to the children. She had noticed one of Sierra's paintings on the back wall—a rendering of a beautiful bird flying away into a blue, clear, and limitless sky.

It was the painting Sierra had started working on the day after her revelation in Dr. Cayden's office. It was her interpretation of freedom. When Steve had finally seen it, he had been so moved he'd told her other people needed to see it. That had sparked a conversation about how she came up with the painting and what it meant to her. That day was the day Sierra shared her past with Steve, and even some of her dreams and her sessions with Dr. Cayden. Steve had been glad she'd trusted him enough to share, and he'd opened up about hurts in his past in turn. In the end, their disclosures had brought them even closer together.

"This painting is amazing, and I think it might inspire the students at the center," Steve had concluded.

That was how it had ended up at the community center—and when the gallery owner saw it, she was moved as well. When she discovered that it was Sierra's painting, she wanted to see more of her work . . . and now, months later, this show was the result of her interest.

A hand coming around her waist and holding her close brought Sierra back to the present. She didn't have to turn around to know who it was. She knew her love's embrace.

"How you doing?" Steve whispered softly in her ear.

Sierra placed her hand over his so they moved even closer together. "I'm wonderful."

"Good. Listen, come with me for a second. I have something for you."

Without hesitation, Sierra took his hand and allowed him to lead her to a room in the back of the gallery where they could be alone.

As they closed the door, Steve took her hands and brought them to his lips. "You know I love you, right?"

Sierra removed one hand from his grasp and gently caressed his face. "I do know. I love you too."

Steve smiled into her eyes. "Close your eyes."

Sierra obeyed, smiled, and waited.

She felt Steve's hands lightly brushing her neck, and déjà vu struck her like a ton of bricks. She felt her body begin to tremble as he finished attaching the clasp on her neck.

"Okay, now open your eyes."

Sierra slowly opened her eyes and looked down. Draped around her neck was a golden heart—the same heart pendant from her dream. *But that was only a dream, wasn't it?* She began to breathe slowly to keep from passing out. Even with her efforts, her body swayed just a little.

Steve held her steady, a concerned expression on his face. "Are you okay?" he asked, drawing her into his body.

Sierra stepped back and looked at Steve, and all the love she felt for him and from him radiated between them. He would never leave her. He would do anything for her. He loved her.

"I'm better than okay," she said. "I have joy and I'm happy."

Acknowledgments

I would like to thank God for everything, including my life and for the inspiration to write *Awaken*. Thank you to everyone who lent their knowledge and expertise to this book. I would also like to thank my family, friends, and everyone who encourages and supports my writing.

About the Author

Denese Shelton has been writing most of her life. She likes to read. She likes to travel. She has a Bachelor of Arts degree in English and a Doctor of Dental Surgery degree. She currently resides in Georgia.

SELECTED TITLES FROM SHE WRITES PRESS

She Writes Press is an independent publishing company
founded to serve women writers everywhere.
Visit us at www.shewritespress.com.

The House on the Forgotten Coast by Ruth Coe Chambers. $16.95,
978-1631523007. When Elise Foster and her parents arrive in
Apalachicola, a fishing village on Florida's northwest coast, in 1987,
the spirit of Annelise Lovett Morgan, who suffered a tragic death on
her wedding day in 1897, comes to Elise asking for help her clear the
name of her true love—merging the past and the present.

Trespassers by Andrea Miles. $16.95, 978-1-63152-903-0. Sexual abuse
survivor Melanie must make a choice: choose forgiveness and begin to
heal from her emotional wounds, or exact revenge for the crimes
committed against her—even if it destroys her family.

A Cup of Redemption by Carole Bumpus. $16.95, 978-1-938314-90-2.
Three women, each with their own secrets and shames, seek to make
peace with their pasts and carve out new identities for themselves.

The Black Velvet Coat by Jill G. Hall. $16.95, 978-1-63152-009-9. When
the current owner of a black velvet coat—a San Francisco artist in
search of inspiration—and the original owner, a 1960s heiress who fled
her affluent life fifty years earlier, cross paths, their lives are forever
changed . . . for the better.

What Is Found, What Is Lost by Anne Leigh Parrish. $16.95,
978-1-938314-95-7. After her husband passes away, a series of family
crises forces Freddie, a woman raised on religion, to confront long-
held questions about her faith.

The Lucidity Project by Abbey Campbell Cook. $16.95,
978-1-63152-032-7. After suffering from depression all her life,
twenty-five-year-old Max Dorigan joins a mysterious research project
on a Caribbean island, where she's introduced to the magical and
healing world of lucid dreaming.

CPSIA information can be obtained
at www.ICGtesting.com
Printed in the USA
BVHW03s1715240718
522456BV00001B/3/P